Nine Open Arms

Jacket and interior art by Dasha Tolstikova

N ederlands
letterenfonds
dutch foundation
for literature

Enchanted Lion Books gratefully acknowledges the support of
the Dutch Foundation for Literature for the translation of this book.
Enchanted Lion Books would also like to thank Mercedes Pritchett for her
always impeccable judgement and Sarah Klinger for precision and great care.

www.enchantedlion.com

First American edition published in 2014 by Enchanted Lion Books,
351 Van Brunt Street, Brooklyn, NY 11231
First published in 2004 in Dutch in the Netherlands by
Em. Querido's Uitgeverij B.V. as *Negen Open Armen*.
Third edition, 2005; fourth edition, 2010; fifth edition, 2011.
Text copyright © 2004 by Benny Lindelauf.
Copyright © 2014 by Enchanted Lion Books for the English (American)
Translation by John Nieuwenhuizen.
Illustrations copyright © 2014 by Enchanted Lion Books
All rights reserved under International and Pan-American Copyright Conventions.
A CIP record is on file with the Library of Congress
Printed in the United States of America by Worzalla, Stevens Point, Wisconsin

Second Printing

Nine Open Arms

Benny Lindelauf

Translated from the Dutch by John Nieuwenhuizen

ENCHANTED LION BOOKS

NEW YORK

For my mother Mia Lindelauf-Boonen,
who gave me a grandmother who
never ran out of stories, and for
Guido Bosua, my friend, who always
wanted to hear her stories.

"Boy, may smoking this cigarette
kill me if it's not true."
– Dien Boonen-Erkens,
storyteller/life artist

CONTENTS

TRANSLATOR'S NOTE

BENNY LINDELAUF, THE AUTHOR of *Nine Open Arms*, was born in 1964 and grew up in the town of Sittard, which is in the province of Limburg in the southeast of the Netherlands. Sittard lies in the narrowest part of Limburg, squeezed between Germany to the east and Belgium to the west. Its location has affected its sometimes tragic history and the lives of the people who lived there. The town in *Nine Open Arms* is modeled on Sittard.

As a child, Lindelauf loved listening to his grandmother's stories. The children in *Nine Open Arms*—four almost adult brothers and three much younger sisters—are "half-orphans," as their mother died some time ago. The responsibility for their upbringing is largely borne by their feisty, but cranky, grandmother, Oma Mei, whose stories they love but often have to beg for. The family struggles to get by, supported by their forever optimistic but often vague father.

The story is built like a jigsaw puzzle and told in stages. It starts in the late 1930s, moves back to the 1860s, and then back to the 1930s. "Nine Open Arms" is the name the family gives to the house they move into in the 1930s. There are many mysteries about the house, its history, and the people—all somehow connected—who have lived there at different times.

In telling this story, Benny Lindelauf sometimes makes his characters use words in colloquial Limburgish to bring the characters, the place, and the times to life. Most of these have been translated into English, but I have kept some of these Limburgish words in the original language because they add to the flavor and liveliness of the story. A glossary of these slang words and a character list follows.

The Dutch often use nicknames, some highly inventive, and few people are known by the often long names first given to them. For example, my "official" name is Johannes Antonius Maria Nieuwenhuizen, but I was always known as Jan, which became John soon after my family of thirteen arrived in Australia from Holland in 1955. The nicknames that appear in the story are also explained in the glossary.

Muulke, the wildest of the three sisters, loves to imagine "tragical tragedies," and Benny Lindelauf has created just that in this heart-warming and often funny, multi-award-winning book.

John Nieuwenhuizen
December 2013

SLANG WORDS
& CHARACTER LIST

Limburgish Slang

iepekriet: shrew, fishwife, hag. (Pronounced: ee-peh-kreet)

kendj: child. (Pronounced: ken-je)

kwatsj: nonsense. (Pronounced: kwa-tch)

leeveke: darling, sweetie. (Pronounced: lay-veh-keh)

miljaar: darn, damn. (Pronounced: mill-yahr)

sjiethoes (plural *sjiethoezer*): coward, chicken. (Pronounced: sheet-hoose)

sjlamm: the wet mixture of coal dust that poor people used to burn because it was cheaper than coal. (Pronounced: sh-lame)

ulezeik: literally "owl's pee," so something insignificant, trivial. (Pronounced: eu-leh-zike)

Principal Characters

THE BOON FAMILY

ANTOON: The children's father. (Pronounced: An-tone)

EET (Short for Etienne): One of the four brothers. (Pronounced: Ate)

FING (Short for Josephine): The narrator and one of the

three sisters.

JESS (Short for Agnes): One of the three sisters. (Pronounced: Yes)

KRIT (Chris in English): One of the four brothers. (Pronounced as written)

MUULKE: (Literally "Little Mouth." As a nickname, it means something like "outspoken" or "bigmouth.") One of the three sisters. (Pronounced: Mule-keh)

OMA MEI (Grandma May in English): The children's maternal grandmother. (Pronounced: Oma My)

OPA PEI (Grandpa Peter in English): The children's maternal grandfather. (Pronounced: Opa Pie)

PIET (Pete in English): One of the four brothers. (Pronounced: Pea-eat)

SJEER: (Gerard in English). One of the four brothers. (Pronounced: Shay-er)

CHARLIE BOTTLETOP: Lame Krit's son and a "Townie."

LAME KRIT (Lame Chris in English): Charlie Bottletop's father.

LEXIDENTLY (LEXI for short): Nienevee's brother, who pronounced "accidentally" as "lexidently," which earned him this nickname.

NIENEVEE: A nickname for a sulky or listless child. One of the Travelers. (Pronounced: Nee-neh-vay)

OOMPAH HATSI: This name is of unclear origin and meaning, though a broom seller of that name is reported to have lived at one time in the city of Sittard. The identity of this character cannot be revealed here. (Pronounced: Um-pah Hat-see)

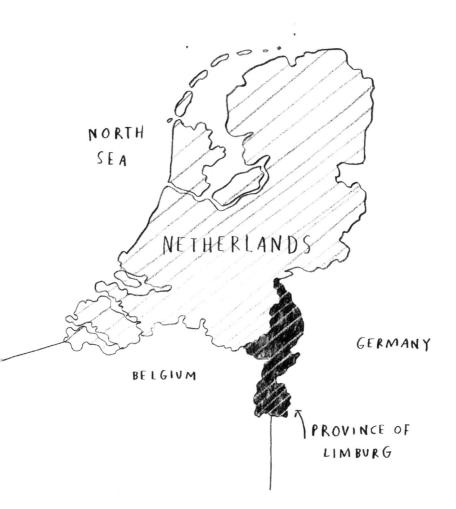

NORTH
SEA

NETHERLANDS

BELGIUM

GERMANY

PROVINCE OF
LIMBURG

PART ONE

Nine Open Arms

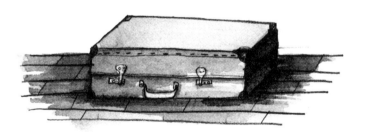

How the House Got Its Name

AT THE END OF Sjlammbams Sahara stood a house. We weren't the first to live there or the first to give the house a name. We had no idea yet about Nienevee from Outside the Walls and Charley Bottletop. But if it hadn't been so windy that day, we surely would have been able to hear them signaling to each other, drumming with their bones deep under the ground.

On the day that we went to inspect the house, there hadn't been a single drop of rain for seven weeks. It was late August 1937, the day after Saint Rosa's Day. A strong, hot wind blew. Dad and our four brothers walked ahead, pushing our large handcart. They had tied handkerchiefs over their noses and mouths to keep out the dust. Not that it was much use, because along with the dust, nasty sharp little stones were being blown about.

Sjlammbams Sahara was a dirt road that continued the paved road leading from the town in the direction of Germany. That long, meandering road had another name, a name nobody could or would remember. We knew, of course, that *sjlamm* was wet coal dust, cheaper to burn than coal. But why this road was nicknamed Sjlammbams Sahara we couldn't say.

With every step, we left the town farther behind. Our grandmother, my sisters, and I walked behind our dad and brothers, listening to their swears. Our middle-sister Muulke filled in the curses that Dad left out. The dust didn't bother us at all. We carried an umbrella the color of lead and amused ourselves by watching our feet move in and out of its shadow.

"Mark my words," Dad shouted. "Once the wind drops, you'll see what a magnificent spot this is!"

"It's mostly a big heap of nothing," Muulke wailed. "And you can't make something from nothing." She nudged me, but I kept quiet.

As we walked, the new cemetery appeared on our left. A row of dense fir trees screened the graves. The trees stood close together and had been so carefully pruned that the row looked like a long straight wall. Compared to Sjlammbams Sahara, which kept veering from left to right and back again, the tight hedge looked a bit like a stern grown-up.

When the road suddenly narrowed into a bumpy pass, Dad encouraged us with his stories. He had to shout to make himself heard above the wind. "Just imagine," he roared, "in autumn this will be carpeted with leaves. And in winter! Frost all over the fields! And gently falling snow will cover the trees! We're going to live in a winter wonderland, believe me!"

It turned out he was dreaming, of course, because no leaf would ever rest on that windswept road for more than a second. In autumn, Sjlammbams Sahara was a river of mud, and winter brought snowstorms and ice-cold, freezing wind. But like so many other things, we didn't know any of that yet.

"Fresh air, as much as you want!" Dad shouted from behind his handkerchief. He listed some other advantages, but gradually he seemed to tire of his own words because his voice grew weaker. The wind snatched his sentences and hid them in the trees. Finally he said, "Why don't you say something, Mother Mei?"

Our grandmother waved him away. Jess, Muulke, and I glanced at each other. Oma Mei didn't usually keep her opinions to herself. For instance, when Dad had announced we would have to move again because of his new job, she had given him a very stern look and had wondered aloud what was wrong with people who stayed in the same profession all their life.

"Opa Pei was an overseer all his life," she'd grumbled. "What's wrong with that for heaven's sake?" She'd added that all this moving might have produced some good stories for the neighbors, but had made tramps of her grandchildren, not to mention herself.

"What are you going to be this time?" she had asked finally, as her swivel-eye pivoted from left to right and her good eye stared at him angrily. We had long since gotten used to her weird eye, but it still could scare a stranger to death.

Dad had kissed the top of her angry head. "Ask what's the opposite of worrying," he'd said.

He couldn't understand why he hadn't thought of it before. It was so obvious. He was going to become a cigar maker. Men were always going to smoke. There was more security in cigars than in silk, which was, after all, a true luxury. And hardware? What could one say in favor of hardware? He named the men he knew who had gone into cigar making and who certainly hadn't done badly since: Nol Rutten, his old school friend. Filip Mols, the undisputed emperor of cigar makers (and, until recently, the only one who had mechanized his business). Then there were Leon Kamps, in Station Street, and Nol Rutten, his old school friend.

"You've already mentioned him," I said.

"Exactly, Fing," said Dad, nearly bursting into song. And hadn't this same Nol Rutten just become the second maker to mechanize, leaving him stuck with old equipment? Two good presses, some twenty cigar molds, and the right sort of knives. Not junk in the least and going for a song. The very same stuff that had helped to make Nol great! If that wouldn't bring good luck! There was just one small problem. Cigars meant we would have to move again, because setting up a cigar factory was not permitted where we lived. It required a separate, sealed space. Only then would a permit be issued. That's what the local council had decided.

"But…" we said.

"No buts, said Dad. "No 'see first, then believe,' but..."

We sighed. "First believe, then see. We know."

"I trust you know where we're moving," Oma Mei had said. And when he told us, her swivel-eye had started spinning.

For Dad to ask us about the opposite of worrying was nothing new.

But his answer was.

Last time, it had been "silk." Before that, "hardware." And every time we objected, he gave the same reply: "First believe, then see."

We had lived in many different places already. There had been the enormous storage loft in the Paardenstraat; the basement of Moffels, the cloth merchant; and our present home, which was a tiny, stuffy three-room house in a lane so narrow that we could reach across it through the first floor window to shake hands with Fie, our neighbor.

During the weeks before our umpteenth move, Jess and Muulke had decided it was war. They'd slammed doors, shaken their fists, and rubbed their eyes, but their hearts hadn't been in it. They were just going through the motions.

I didn't complain. I'd known already that sooner or later we'd have to move again. Like always. We were globetrotters within our own town. North, south, east, west: we were able to go everywhere but didn't feel at home anywhere, and now it seemed we were about to move again.

Along with which, we'd also have to go to a new school. "Because it's closer," said Oma Mei, which was nonsense, of course, since it was barely an extra ten minutes' walk to our old school, but Oma saw an opportunity to finally get us into the convent school of the Ursuline nuns. It was a much stricter school than our old one and the headmistress was Oma Mei's old school friend.

"We all have to like the place, of course," said Dad. As if we didn't know he had rented it on the spot, afraid someone would beat him to it. Never mind that the house had been empty for years.

When the road emerged from the pass, the house came into view and we stopped. Only our brothers kept walking. They were deep in conversation about the future. From the way they were gesturing, I could tell they already saw themselves getting rich.

"Do they think the house is even farther?" I wondered aloud.

"Farther than this, nothing even exists," Muulke said, sounding quite upset.

From where we were standing, Sjlammbams Sahara took one more sharp turn, and then there was nothing. The road did continue across the border, but there was nothing in front of us that had a street name. This was where names came to an end. This was where the world came to an end. And it only started up again a seeming infinity of wheat fields later, where Germany began.

"Our house," announced Dad, untying his handkerchief.

"At the end of the world!" Muulke moaned. Less than an hour ago she had made fun of Fie because she was going to have to spend the rest of her life in a tiny upstairs apartment, while we were going to live in a real house. Nothing much was left of that triumph now. Muulke, who usually looked like a doll, with thick doll's hair and doll's eyes with doll's eyelashes, now looked rather like a goblin, with wild tufts of hair sticking out everywhere.

"Can you see the graveyard?" Jess asked fearfully. She was the only one still taking shelter behind the umbrella. "Please tell me you can't see any of it."

"I can see the dead waving at us," said Muulke. "Boo!"

Jess tried to stick her fingers in her ears and to hang on to the umbrella at the same time, but it didn't work. A gust of wind hurled the thing into the air and sent it tumbling along Sjlammbams Sahara.

"Well?" asked Dad. "Well?"

In front of us, half-hidden by trees and shrubs, rose a wide, red brick wall. Right at the top were two tiny attic windows, the size of tea towels. Then nothing for a long stretch, but down below, among the tall weeds, there were two little cellar windows. A few bricks in the wall were crumbling and sat at odd angles.

"Well?" Dad said again.

I stared at the wall, trying to think of the right words.

"Where's the front door?" asked Jess.

For a moment I thought Dad would search in his pockets absentmindedly, the way he always did when he'd lost something. We stood staring at the wall. There was no front door, or any other kind of door, even though this side of the house definitely faced the road.

"Around the corner," we heard Piet call.

We rounded the corner and stopped. Was that supposed to be the front door? Those few slats covered in flaking green paint with a doorhandle hanging loose? There were some small windowpanes in the center, though one was broken.

The key didn't fit the lock.

"I can't understand it…" Dad looked from the key to the lock and back again.

It was Piet who called again. "The next corner!"

And there was the front door: a proper front door of solid oak with a peephole and a brass doorknob with dents in it. The only thing that spoiled the effect was four holes in the wall, just above the door.

And now the key did fit—if only you could reach it, considering the bottom of the door was at knee height.

"They must have been worried about floods," Piet grinned.

The next thing we knew, our four brothers—Piet, Eet, Sjeer, and Krit—were climbing inside with exaggerated groans and breathlessness.

"A front door at the back, a threshold at knee-height," Dad said cheerfully. "Is this a house full of surprises or what?"

We walked through the hallway. The window shutters were still closed and the only light we had came through the stained glass fanlight above the door. It was as if the floor was covered in diamonds and sapphires.

Four doors led off the hall. "We've never had so many doors all to ourselves," we whispered to each other, without even meaning to whisper.

At the end of the hallway, a broad stairway with carved banisters led up to the first floor.

"Are we allowed up there?" Jess asked doubtfully.

Muulke clacked her tongue. "Of course, *sjiethoes*," she said. "The whole house is ours." She raced up the stairs but stopped abruptly when, halfway up, a step suddenly gave way with a loud moaning sound.

"And this is your room," said Dad.

Jess, Muulke, and I gasped.

"Our room? For us? Just us?"

The walls were whitewashed and the wood floor was bare, as if the room was somehow waiting to be ours. When we were living in the storage loft, Dad had made a room for us by hanging curtains from the rafters. But this was a real room with a real window! We tried to open it but couldn't get it to budge.

"That's for later," said Dad.

Later, when we were all sitting in the living room and coffee was bubbling on the kerosene stove we'd hauled along, it suddenly felt as if we were already living in the house, even though there was a large crack in the living room wall and the splintered floorboards were full of holes. Still, the house was airy and smelled safe.

By the end of the afternoon, Oma Mei, tired of being cranky, sat down on Dad's overcoat. She leaned crookedly against the wall and snored straight through all the first words of all the first sentences in our new house. The left side of her wrinkled face was white with plaster from the wall.

"If Oma Mei can sleep here, anyone can," said Dad.

And he carefully wiped the whitewash from his mother-in-law's cheek with his handkerchief.

When we were back in our old first-floor apartment that evening, we solemnly shook hands through the kitchen window with Fie, the girl who lived opposite. Muulke cried, then Jess cried, and finally I did, too.

Fie's parents gave us a jar of cherries preserved in brandy. "To celebrate."

"Nothing much to celebrate for a while yet," said Oma Mei somberly. "But thank you all the same."

The next few weeks were a wild whirlwind of work and dust! The dust swirled everywhere as the furniture, one heavy piece at a time, was heaved across the high threshold, with much swearing. When everything was finally in place, Oma Mei covered her face with her hands and wept, "Just look at us! Just look at us now!"

We couldn't understand why she was crying, but we comforted her anyway. We stood together in the main room—Oma Mei, Dad, our brothers, Muulke, Jess, and I—looking at our nine chairs and our round table, which formed a little island in a sea of bare floorboards.

Muulke, Jess, and I tried to work out how long the room was by standing next to each other, legs and arms spread wide till our fingers hurt from stretching. Starting at the front of the room, we each had to take three turns before reaching the back wall.

"Three times three makes nine," said Jess.

And there were nine of us.

"A real coincidence!" I said.

But Muulke said it had nothing to do with coincidence.

"I think…" she said.

"Don't tell me," said Jess. She stared at Muulke with a look I knew only too well. Her eyes looked greedy and scared at the same time. I knew what was coming.

"Stop it," I said.

"I think…" said Muulke.

Of the five houses we had lived in over the past four years, three had been cursed and the other two had at least "traces of a tragical tragedy." Or that's what Muulke had decided.

"Something to do with a gruesome murder," Muulke said this time. "With knives and blood and all that."

Jess stuck her fingers in her ears. Muulke shaped her hands into a horn and yelled that the holes above the front door were evidence enough. They were bullet holes, of course. And the graveyard wasn't so close by for nothing.

Oma Mei sailed into the room, gave Muulke a smack, and sent us off to town to buy wallpaper for the living room.

"Did you have to do that?" I asked.

"At least I say what I think," said Muulke, still holding her hand over her cheek.

"Blabbermouth," I threw at her.

"*Iepekriet!*"

We walked down Sjlammbams Sahara. Jess was nine, Muulke ten, and I was eleven.

"Do you think Oma Mei will unpack the Crocodile this

time?" asked Jess.

Muulke nodded. Without looking back, she held out her hand to me and we automatically linked arms. Just in case it did depend on us, we chanted to the rhythm of our footsteps, "Unpack, unpack, unpack."

We looked back. Through the open windows we could hear Oma Mei's carpetbeater attacking the carpets. The wind had died down a bit. We could even hear a blackbird.

When we entered Mr. Walraven's paint shop, we told him why we had come. But when he asked us how much wallpaper we needed, we stared at each other blankly.

"*Miljaar*!" said Muulke.

"We forgot to measure," I said.

Jess didn't even blink. "That one will do."

"But how much do you need?" Mr. Walraven wanted to know.

Without even hesitating, Jess replied, "We'll take nine open arms."

"You're a genius," said Muulke, and the three of us roared with laughter at Mr. Walraven's mystified face.

"We'll show you," I said.

We started at the back of the cramped little shop, among the rolls of wallpaper and tins of whitewash. Three times three in a row, with arms spread wide. Mr. Walraven measured, shaking his head, pencil behind his ear, until we stood outside between the milk cart and a horse-drawn carriage.

Then Mr. Walraven, who liked a joke, wrote on the sales slip: WALLPAPER MEASURING NINE OPEN ARMS @ 45¢ PER ARM.

And that is how our house got its name.

Gruesome Treasure

AT THE END OF Sjlammbams Sahara stood a house. We went to live in that house and gave it a name: Nine Open Arms. That must have been the right name, because the house gave us something in return. Or rather, it gave Muulke something.

"Why her?" Jess complained. "The name was my idea, wasn't it?"

"Stop being so prickly," said Muulke. "You would have dropped dead on the spot with fright, anyway."

Two months had passed by the time Muulke made her discovery. The living room had been wallpapered, and the Belgian potbelly stove with the shutter (the one Muulke insisted used to belong to a witch who burnt babies) stood scrubbed and polished in the back of the room. Oma Mei was on her knees with a dustpan and a broom, trying to sweep the sand out of the cracks between the floorboards, but the minute she'd swept it out of one crack, it would disappear into the next. She looked hot and annoyed. Her neck was red, her knuckles white.

"Go get some *sjlamm*," she told Muulke.

"But I had to do it yesterday."

"Muulke…"

"Can't Fing do it?"

"She's in the garden."

"And Jess?"

"The bucket is in the hall."

"Jess never has to do anything," Muulke muttered.

"I could box your ears," Oma Mei threatened. She shifted and sand crunched under her knees.

Muulke picked up the bucket, lit the kerosene lamp, and headed down the ramshackle wooden stairs to the cellar.

Nine Open Arms had three cellars. The first was the storeroom, which was where potatoes and onions were kept. There were also two sets of shelves holding preserved vegetables and fruit. The bright-blue preserving jar with cherries in brandy had a lonely spot on the top shelf. The second cellar was for storing coal and *sjlamm*. The third, right at the back of the basement, was forbidden territory. We had only ever been there once, when we were inspecting the house.

"Don't ever let me catch you going there," Oma Mei had warned.

Hidden behind that last, rusty iron door lay a random collection of stuff: stacks of horse blankets, crates of big-bellied green bottles, an armchair with three legs, a sour-smelling beer barrel. Things were stacked higgledy-piggledy, often covered with horse blankets. Dad had promised at leaset ten times to clear it all out.

Once in the storeroom, Muulke went through the stone archway that led to the second cellar. There lay the *sjlamm*, like an enormous black pudding on a bed of wood shavings.

"What if that mouse hadn't been there?" Jess often said later.

"What if it had been there," I'd reply, "but it hadn't run over Muulke's foot?"

"What if I'd worn closed shoes instead of open sandals?" Muulke would add.

"Then you wouldn't have felt that mouse."

"Then you wouldn't have been scared to death."

"Then you wouldn't have dropped the bucket."

"Then maybe nothing would have happened at all."

It's amazing how close some stories get to never being born at all.

If you drop a bucket on top of a heap of old *sjlamm* it won't matter very much because that *sjlamm* will be rock hard. But that morning the coalman had delivered fresh *sjlamm*, and it was a soft, thick mush. So when the bucket fell, a fat blob of it splattered onto Muulke's dress. Muulke groaned. If there was one thing Oma Mei couldn't stand it was dirty clothes, especially on Tuesdays, because that meant she had to wash them again after having spent all of Monday at the washtub.

There was nothing Muulke could use to clean up her dress in the first and second cellars, so she went looking.

Carefully, she opened the iron door of the third cellar. At the back there were two small arched windows. There was no glass in them, so the air wasn't as musty as it had been in the second cellar. Muulke looked around. The spooky atmosphere didn't come so much from the actual things as from all those things being covered in blankets, so they looked like strange, lumpy things with lots of hollows and things sticking out.

The bottles in the crates were empty, so there was nothing with which to clean. But then Muulke thought of the horse blankets.

"To wipe off that lump of *sjlamm*," she said later.

The nearest blanket covered a large, flat object. The instant she touched the blanket, it slid down, as if it had been expecting this touch for years. The blanket turned out to be much heavier than she'd expected, and it slipped through her fingers to the floor. When the dust had settled, she saw it.

She saw what the house was giving us.

"Believe me," Muulke said whenever Jess started going on about it not being fair. "You would have peed in your pants three times over."

We were still half-standing at the kitchen table, petrified by Muulke's scream from below, when she came hurtling up the steps and stormed into the kitchen.

"A tombstone!" she screamed. "A tombstone!"

We all held our breath. Oma Mei pressed one finger to the lid of her wildly fluttering swivel-eye and stared at Muulke in her dirty, torn dress, without a bucket of *sjlamm*.

"Maria Catharina Alfonsa Theodora Boon, haven't you forgotten something?"

Her voice had a soft, dangerous tone, but Muulke wasn't one to notice tones.

"I knew it!" She wriggled in between Jess and me and cut herself a piece of bread. "A tragical tragedy, didn't I tell you? A tombstone in the cellar! You have to see it!"

"That isn't a tombstone," said Oma Mei.

"It is so," said Muulke with her mouth full. "A stone with skulls and everything! In our cellar! Come and see!"

"Nobody goes anywhere," Oma Mei snapped.

"I can feel a sermon coming on," Eet muttered to Sjeer.

We knew better than to disobey our grandmother.

"Thank God your mother never had to bring you up herself," said Oma Mei halfway through her sermon. Our dead mother belonged in her rants the way a brass band belongs in a parade. "What would have become of you? She always had a heart as soft as a rag doll."

As always, her eyes filled with tears at these words.

We tried to comfort her, Muulke most of all, but Oma Mei resisted all pats, strokes, and kisses. Still, she was a little gentler afterwards. Not that she would allow us to go and look in the cellar. "Nobody has any business down there," she said.

That afternoon, Jess, Muulke, and I were outside in what once had been a vegetable garden. Now it was full of weeds. Only here and there did we find an overgrown leek or a sprouting onion.

The sky was covered with heavy clouds. It had been like that for days, but there hadn't been a drop of rain. We could see Sjlammbams Sahara through the gate. The road looked gray and miserable. I bent over and pulled at weeds that wouldn't come out.

"Oma Mei is a sourpuss," said Muulke, who was weeding with me.

"She's just having a bad day," I said.

"Let me try," said Jess.

"No," Muulke and I said together.

"But I know how to do it," said Jess.

"Don't whine," I said, but in a friendly tone.

Jess leaned angrily against the gate.

"And—she—just—doesn't—like—moving," Muulke panted while she and I kept pulling.

With a dry crack, the weed broke off. We nearly fell over backwards. We looked at the spot where the weed had been. The roots had stayed behind.

"*Miljaar!*" said Muulke.

"If you'd let me do it, it would have come out properly," said Jess.

"Anyway, it isn't true that she dislikes moving," I said.

"Have you forgotten about the Crocodile?" asked Muulke. "Have you forgotten how she carried on with Dad?"

"That was because she hates leaving places."

"But that's what moving is, isn't it?" asked Muulke.

"That's one part of it," I said. "The other part is arriving somewhere, starting over."

My sisters looked at me.

"I hadn't thought about it that way," said Muulke.

I hadn't either. Sometimes I just said things before I'd even thought about or understood them.

"I still don't see the difference," said Jess.

"Oma Mei doesn't dislike making a fresh start," I said. "Whenever we've moved, she's always been the first to pick up the thread. 'Don't whine,' she says, and …"

"'Just think of Oompah Hatsi,'" Muulke and Jess finished.

That sentence, which we knew by heart, was about our neighbor Oompah Hatsi from across the road three houses ago (when Dad had bought a supply of wicker baskets to trade, all of which turned out to have rotting bottoms). Oompah was an elderly dealer in buttons and haberdashery. He was thrown out onto the street when, for the umpteenth time, he couldn't pay his rent.

But Oompah didn't take it lying down and turned the street into his home. At first as a form of protest, later because his protest had no effect and he had to live somewhere.

Fortunately, he was evicted in June, when the days were already getting warmer. He put his bed in the covered dead-end alley next to the butcher's shop. He washed in the water bucket the milkman kept for his horse, and he always took great care with his appearance. His reddish-gray hair was combed back tightly, and his chin and cheeks, he declared, were "smooth as a pebble from the river, just have a feel."

One day, Oompah hung up pictures on the walls of the alley—or rather picture frames, because the pictures were no longer in them. What you saw were framed pieces of wall: a framed crack, a hole in the wall. It was as if you suddenly had a completely new view of the street you lived in. When Oompah realized we liked the frames, he started moving them around so that he had something new to show us all the time.

"Jess, Fing, Muu-huulke! Look! Sleeping Spider in a Web."

"Jess, Fing, Muu-huu-huulke! Speckled Mushroom on the Wall."

"Jess, Fing, Muu-huu-huulke! Take a good look! Look really hard!"

Jess said he sounded like a wolf when he cried "Muu-huu-huulke."

For a while, all went well. From his spot in the alley, he repaired clothes for money, and with his nimble fingers he was able to turn any old rag into something wearable.

When summer passed and the weather turned cold, though, Oompah Hatsi started drinking. He was what people call a nasty drunk. At night he kept the whole neighborhood awake with his yelling. He was thrown out of the cafe where he always went because he sneakily cut buttons off other customers' coats. One night, he ate those buttons. The police came and took him away to the madhouse.

"Totally deranged, the poor soul," Oma Mei said after, with her hand over her mouth. "Ready for the asylum."

We had no idea what "deranged" meant, or what an "asylum" was, but we figured they had something to do with Oompah Hatsi's button-eating and his terrible screaming that night, when his tongue bled hideously from chewing the buttons. For a whole month after that, Jess had nightmares about being chased by a large howling wolf with a bleeding tongue. "Jess, Fing, Muu-huulke! Have a good look! Jess, Fing, Muu-huu-huulke! Look really hard!"

Muulke and I worked on in silence. A bunch of weeds broke off at the root. I had blisters on my hands.

"We need a spade," we told Dad.

"A spade? What for?"

"Oma Mei told us to pull out the weeds."

"You can pull out weeds for the rest of your life."

"But Oma Mei said…" I grumbled.

"Stop blabbing," said Muulke, quickly dragging me away.

The rest of the afternoon we played Threatened Treasure. One of us was the house, another the treasure hidden inside, and the third the threat. I was usually the house because Muulke had no talent for standing still. That afternoon she was first a savage soldier, then an all-consuming fire, and finally an all-devouring monster. In the end, she became all of these at once and danced furiously around the house (me). Her hands were at once flames and claws, but she couldn't get at the treasure. I made very sure of that.

"You're a dead-boring house," Muulke complained.

"And you cheat," objected Jess, who was hanging onto my

dress, her eyes squeezed shut. "You can only be one threat at a time." She wanted to change parts, to show how it really should be done.

"You can't be the threat," said Muulke.

"Can too."

"Can't."

"Can."

"A threat must be able to sneak up, you know that."

"I can sneak up perfectly well!" shouted Jess.

"But you have to be able to do it really quietly."

"I can!"

"But you squeak and creak."

"I don't!"

"I can hear you."

"You can't."

"Squeak. Creak. Squeak. Creak."

"Fing! She says I squeak-creak."

It was hard work calming them both down. I managed, but it meant the end of the game. We climbed up on the fence in front of the house. Jess wanted to know what sort of rags our mother's heart had been made of.

"You know perfectly well what Oma Mei meant."

Jess swore solemnly that she didn't know. It nearly brought tears to her eyes. I gave her my hanky. Of course she knew, but she never passed up a chance to hear more about our mother.

"Oma Mei means she had a gentle character," I said. "That she couldn't say no. That she went along with everything."

"Everything?" said Jess.

"Everything," I said.

"Everything squeak, everything creak," said Muulke.

"Fi-hing!"

"Now stop it, both of you!"

A million years ago, we'd had a mother. Oma Mei always said she was so nice that everybody who used to know her still came close to tears when they spoke of her.

She'd died three months after Jess was born. Oma Mei said it was her heart and that a rag-doll heart doesn't last long in this world. "That's not hard to see," she'd always say. "You have to be hard in this world, and it's not for nothing that 'heart' and 'hard' sound so much alike."

We heard whistling. Our brothers were coming outside, all four of them, each with a cigar in his mouth. When they got closer we saw that their cigars were fakes, made from leftover strips of living room wallpaper.

"Need any big brothers?"

I showed them my blistered hands and complained that they could have come a bit sooner. Muulke shook her doll's head sadly and said that the witch of the Belgian potbelly stove had just murdered her and it was too late to be rescued.

Our brothers wept crocodile tears and carried her high above their heads with their strong arms. The murder victim peered through her doll's eyelashes to see if we were watching from behind, but, of course, we made sure we weren't.

That evening, when we were in our bedroom, we could hear Dad and Oma Mei's muffled voices. We crept out of bed and pushed aside the rug in the middle of the room where there was a narrow crack in the boards. Light from the living room below shone through it. The crack was too narrow for us to be able to see anything, but big enough for us to hear their voices clearly.

"…have cleaned that up ages ago," said Oma Mei. "Now see what's come of it."

"I've been busy," said Dad.

"*Kwatsj!*"

"Setting up a cigar workshop is no *ulezeik*."

"Did you tell the girls they didn't have to do the weeding?"

"They'll have plenty of time for working."

"Do you want them to become good-for-nothings?"

"A bit of play won't do them any harm!"

Angry footsteps pounded across the living room floor. Then we heard the sloshing of water being scooped from the bucket in the kitchen and poured into the kettle. There was silence for a while. We kneeled on the floor in our nightgowns. It was late October and the nights were already frosty. After sitting still for ten minutes, we were blue with cold. We could hear chairs being moved about, and the aroma of coffee rose up through the crack. It was a delicious aroma, the sort that made us want to be downstairs. But we knew that if we went, we'd never find out why Oma Mei was acting so strangely. So we ignored the aroma, the cold, and our sore knees.

"We should never have come here," said Oma Mei.

"But we absolutely had to get out of there," said Dad.

"You can't fool me, Antoon. You're not fooling anybody. The only person you're fooling—"

"Oh, come on, Mother Mei—"

"—is yourself. Of all the places you could have chosen..."

"There wasn't much to choose from."

"Of all places, you had to pick this one?"

"It's a large house. There's a vegetable garden. And separate bedrooms for the boys and the girls. Right. I can see what you mean."

"Watch out, Antoon Boon." There was a sharp edge to her voice.

Dad gave a deep sigh. "I'm sorry."

"Bringing up those children is no *ulezeik* either."

"I'm sorry."

"And all the while I'm already standing with one-and-a-half feet in my grave."

"I'm sorry."

"And then you have to go and choose this house, of all houses."

"What is the matter with this house?" Dad asked.

"I can only hope that it's found rest."

"Who's found rest?" asked Dad.

There was no answer. We heard nothing more. Just the ticking of the cuckoo clock and the bubbling of the kettle on the fire. Above us, the wind rustled through the gaps between the roof tiles, making a rumbly sound.

I was the first to give up and go back to bed. Then Jess snuggled up to me, shivering. Finally, Muulke got up stiffly. She threw back the blankets angrily, crawled into bed, and sat up straight. The sheet came untucked and let in a cold draft. Jess groaned.

"Something has happened here," said Muulke.

"Yes, a tragical tragedy." I yawned.

"Go to sleep," said Jess.

But Muulke stared stubbornly into the darkness, her eyes glittering.

The Tomb in the Cellar

THE STAIRS CREAKED WHEN Oma Mei and Dad came upstairs. We lay shivering in a knot of ice-cold arms and legs. Outside, the wind howled. A storm was blowing. The moon broke through the clouds, throwing a blue glow over the bedspread. The metal knobs on our rickety old bed lit up. In the quiet, we could hear Dad settling into his bed. There was a grumbly sigh, then a long silence.

"Can I go soft?" asked Jess.

"No," Muulke and I said together.

"Just for a little while."

"No, you're not allowed."

"Why not?"

"You know why not."

Jess started gasping.

I sighed.

"Don't give in," said Muulke.

"I'm not giving in."

Jess started gasping even worse.

"It's not for nothing that 'heart' and 'hard' sound so

similar," Muulke said.

"For how long?" I asked.

"Just ten minutes."

"Five," said Muulke.

"You should stay out of this," said Jess and changed places with me before Muulke could object.

Our bed had been specially made. The outer parts each had a long mattress filled with wool. Muulke and I slept on those. The middle part had only a wooden bottom with a woolen blanket over it. That was Jess's place because she needed to lie flat.

Jess had a vertebra that moved, became dislocated. You couldn't see it, only feel it, which was easiest with closed eyes. The vertebra sat at the level of her shoulder blades. If it slipped out, she had terrible pain in her back, and sometimes she couldn't even walk. When that happened, the vertebra had to be pushed back in, and then she had to lie flat on her back for a long time.

When we first found out about it, two years ago, Muulke and I competed to see who could find it fastest. We became experts and could do it even faster than the doctors who examined Jess.

On the very day it had been diagnosed, Oma Mei had walked all the way to Maastricht to get Jess a corset, which was called a "straightener."

"That's not a backbone you've got, it's a wreckbone," she'd said dryly when she returned home late that evening. The sole of her left shoe had come loose and flapped with every step she took.

Jess cried for a week about that straightener. It was an ugly sausage-like tube with leather straps that had to be tightened. At the back were wooden slats, which went on either side of her backbone. She had to wear it during the day. Jess thought it was horrible, particularly when she discovered that the leather and the buckles squeaked and creaked if she moved too fast. Only when Oma Mei said that without it she would grow as crooked as a capital letter C, did she stop resisting.

Muulke got up and put on a sweater.

"What are you going to do?" I whispered.

"You know what."

Jess said that getting up was the last thing in the world she was going to do.

"Jess is right," I said, but before I knew it I had my sweater on, and Jess followed, as always.

We crept past Oma Mei's door, which stood ajar, and went down the stairs. The house creaked and groaned.

"Mind the sixth," whispered Muulke. "Mind the sixth."

We skipped the squealing step.

Behind the door that led into the cellar, the dark was as pitch-black as fresh *sjlamm*. Muulke went in front with the smoking kerosene lamp.

"I'm not going one step farther," said Jess.

"She's right," I said, but Muulke dragged me along after her, so all I could do was grab Jess's hand, too. The three of us went down the cellar steps together. We went farther and farther down. It felt as if we were descending to the center of the earth.

Something strange happens to smells at night. It's as if the night polishes them up and every smell seems sharp and clear. The muddy smell of the potatoes, the musty smell of the horse blankets, and, far away, the thin smell of beer. And then there was the smell of something that wasn't anything in particular: the cellar smelled of time past.

In the flickering light of the first cellar, the preserve jars looked like they were floating. We hung on to each other as we went. We bumped our knees, our shoulders, our heads; we heard strange rustling and scratching sounds; but we kept hanging on to each other.

"I'm going back," whispered Jess. "I'm really going back, right now."

"Go on then," grumbled Muulke. "Go on upstairs, *sjiethoes*."

I felt Jess's hand clasping my wrist like a small claw. I tried to loosen her fingers. What on earth were we doing here? Why on earth had I come along? I could have just stayed behind in my bed, couldn't I? Shivering, I moved forward into the pitch-black hole that led into the third cellar. Muulke stumbled, nearly dropping the lamp. Then we stood motionless because Jess thought she had heard Oma Mei.

"What did you really hear?"

"I don't know. Something."

Our hearts were thumping as we stood and listened. We didn't know which we'd rather believe: that it had been Oma Mei, or the opposite. Because if it wasn't her, then who or what was it? Underground, it was still, dark, and icy cold.

"This is what it's like when you're dead," said Muulke.

"Blabbermouth," I said, but I heard my voice trembling.

Muulke handed me the lantern and opened the door to the third cellar.

In the shadowy light, all those strange objects seemed to be floating around again, and they seemed far more creepy than all the stuff in the first and second cellars combined. Since we had no idea what was what, each thing could be anything.

"You're squashing my hand," said Jess.

In the back stood an enormous old weather-beaten mirror. The top edge of the frame was missing. The mirror was covered with black spots, so our mirror images looked as if they'd gotten lost in a black snowstorm. We stared at ourselves—at the sweaters over our nightgowns and at our pale faces, full of strange, sharp shadows.

"We look as if we've been through something frightful." Muulke's voice sounded weird and high.

"Hurry up," Jess squeaked. "Where's that tombstone?"

Muulke pointed.

Jess and I took the tiniest little step closer. And then another.

"Didn't you say it was a gravestone?" I said.

"With skulls and everything?" said Jess.

"That's what I thought," said Muulke, looking confused.

Because what we saw was the headboard of a bed. True, it was a strange headboard, and it really did look like a tombstone with its round arch. Inside the arch, a border had been carved out, and two dates had been carved into the wood:

AUGUST 30, 1863–JULY 7, 1870

But we could clearly see the legs of the bed, so it was just a headboard, nothing else.

"Come on, let's go now," I said.

"Wait," said Muulke, holding the lantern closer. "There's more writing." She brushed away a thick layer of cobwebs. "Niene... Nienev..."

"Nienevee," said Jess. "It says Nienevee."

"Is that the person who has to find rest?" asked Muulke.

I sighed crossly. Wasn't it completely idiotic for us to be staring at an old bed in the middle of the night? We weren't little children any more, were we?

"It's ridiculous," I mumbled.

And that's when we heard the first "Arghh!" And that first "Arghh!" came from under the ground.

Many memories change over time, but that "Arghh!" coming from under the ground has never changed. It sounded muffled, as if it had to force its way up through the earth, and then up through the concrete of the cellar floor.

"Aaarghhhh!"

It was a terrifying, croaking, moaning sound.

"It's the wind," I said.

But if it was the wind, why did I suddenly jump back? Why was I suddenly standing on a chair? Why did the floor of the cellar feel as fragile as an eggshell, as if at any moment something terrible could come up through it? Jess grabbed me and hung on tight. The chair creaked and wobbled. I jumped off and landed on Jess's heel, and she kicked Muulke's shin in her fright. We all jumped back.

"Ohgodohgodohgod," Jess squeaked. "There!! Look, there!"

Somehow we had managed to scramble back to the first cellar. Muulke swung the lantern around, and our shadows moved all around us, too. Even the glass jars of preserved fruit on the shelf next to us began to look sinister. As if the light-red cherries and the white pears weren't fruits at all, but something else, something…

"Something deadish," whispered Jess.

Then came the second "Aaaarghhhhh!" even more drawn-out and disconsolate than the first.

I scraped my head against the ceiling. Muulke hit Jess's chin with the lantern. We tripped over each other trying to get upstairs. We never could work out how we managed to get out of that cellar without doing each other mortal injury. Nor how we eventually got back upstairs and into our bed, gasping for breath, our hearts thumping, without even taking off our sweaters or waking Oma Mei.

But there was one thing I knew for sure: it was all very well to think we'd grown too old for certain things, but those things, whatever they were, obviously didn't agree.

The Opposite of Worrying [1]

NEXT MORNING, ON NOL Rutten's handcart, the opposite of worrying arrived: three heavy sacks packed in straw matting and a stack of five crates.

"This is for the fillers," said Nol, pointing at the sacks.

"The fillers," said Dad.

"And the wrappers are in those crates."

Dad looked from the sacks to the crates, casually repeating everything Nol said. His eyes were shining.

"And these are the presses. This one here needs a drop of oil, but the other one is tiptop."

"A drop of oil. Of course," said Dad.

In the back of the cart lay a stack of wooden molds with rounded slits. Our brothers unloaded everything. Meanwhile, Oma Mei told Nol she really hoped he wasn't taking his old friend for a ride, because she would strongly resent that, especially since she had to look after all these half-orphans, as he could well see. In the same breath, she told him that half-orphans counted for as much as whole orphans, since sorrow is sorrow, after all, and it can't be divided in two. She certainly wasn't complaining about the fact that she, the widow of a supervisor, had to keep a whole family going while she already stood with one-and-a-half feet in her grave, but bringing up children was no *ulezeik*, and would he like a piece of fruit pie?

Nol said she was absolutely right and yes, thank you, he would have some pie; no, not the plum jam one, which would be a bit filling at this time of day, but the apple. He found Oma Mei's sharp tongue easier to bear than Dad's looks of doggish devotion.

"Don't go on about it," Nol said to Dad a bit later, when he and Dad stood by the side of the road. "I let you pay. Well and truly!"

Then he took off.

Muulke, Jess, and I watched our brothers trying to turn the screw of the unoiled press. Piet and Eet on one side, Krit and Sjeer on the other, their faces red, their cheeks puffed out.

"Are you children still here?" Oma Mei worried. "Hurry up, off to school!"

We ran down Sjlammbams Sahara, with Oma Mei's warning not to run and to stay together still ringing in our ears. We ran as far as the market. We stopped there to straighten each other's hair ribbons and waited for Jess to catch her breath.

"Am I still squeak-creaking?" asked Jess.

"No."

"Listen really hard," she said.

"We are listening! We are!" we promised. "You're as silent as a mouse."

Luckily, we arrived just in time. The classes hadn't lined up yet.

I didn't really miss our old school. It had been a small,

untidy building of only three rooms, and the headmistress was stone-deaf. But I still had to force myself to walk on to the playground of our new school. Jess was even more timid. Muulke, on the other hand, had marched up to a group of girls on the very first day and was skipping rope with them in less than a minute.

That morning, we had different classes, where we rattled off multiplication tables, parsed sentences, and recited from the catechism. I waited impatiently for recess, sure that Muulke was going to talk about last night and that she was going to make Jess even more scared than she already was.

"It was the wind," I said as soon as we were together, before Muulke could even open her mouth. We were standing in the gloomy little courtyard below the statue of Mary, which looked just as disheveled as the rest of the building. "It was the wind, and that's all there is to it."

"The wind doesn't say 'Arghh!'" said Muulke. "And certainly not from under the ground."

"It only sounded like it came from under the ground," I said.

"For sure?"

"Yes."

"You knew it then?"

"Of course," I said.

"Oh, yeah? Then why did you jump four feet into the air?"

"Because you were making me nervous," I replied.

"I tell you, there's something down there," said Muulke. "I swear it. And that Niene... eh..."

"Nienevee," said Jess.

"That Nienevee has something to do with it."

"A tragical tragedy, of course," I said. "Now just stop it. There's nothing the matter with that house and there's nothing the matter with that cellar."

Jess looked from me to Muulke, like a hungry little stray dog that's offered two sausages and doesn't know which one to choose.

After school, we waited for each other outside St. Michael's Church on the market square. Fie, who used to be our neighbor, walked with us as far as the Putse Gate. From there, she solemnly waved us off out of the town, the way she'd done every day since we'd moved. And we waved back, leaving the town's walls behind. We felt brave and forlorn at the same time.

At the beginning of Sjlammbams Sahara there were still a few houses: a farm belonging to Mr. Wetsels, who also owned the field next to our house; opposite, diagonally, the whitewashed house of "Nose" Hermes; and the third and last farm along the road was Farmer Kalle's. Beyond that, there was nothing.

The closer to winter we got, the bigger this nothing seemed. Once the grain had been harvested and the beets had been pulled up, the undulating land became bleaker and more bare. In the end, all that was left were the furrows made by the ploughs, like a promise for the New Year.

Since we'd moved, Oma Mei seemed more determined than ever to prevent us all from becoming good-for-nothings. The windows had to be washed. The laundry had to be soaked, scrubbed, and put through the wringer. The straw mattresses our brothers slept on had to be shaken and their blankets aired. Even the coal corner in the cellar had to be scrubbed clean once a week. And the floor with the cracks had to be swept, and swept again.

"It's as if the sand is constantly creeping out of it," Muulke complained. She was down on her knees and was sweeping so wildly that the dust flew in all directions, making my nose itch. She glared at Jess who was sticking new labels on preserving jars.

"Why don't you ever have to do anything?" she grumbled.

"I am doing something, aren't I?" said Jess. "Fing, aren't I doing something?"

"Yes, you are."

"But we do more," said Muulke. She looked at me. The large ribbon in her hair was half undone. "Fing, don't we do more?"

"We don't have a wreckbone."

"She's just faking."

"Muulke says I'm faking," cried Jess.

"She's not faking," I said sternly.

I was glad when Oma Mei called for me.

Every day, we had to get water from the pump in the new cemetery because the well next to our house produced only muddy slush. We had an old baby carriage whose cradle had been removed. In its place, Dad had put a wooden platform with two zinc tubs, which was where the water went.

I pushed the carriage ahead of me. On the other side of the road there was a gap in the hedge. It wasn't an official town entrance to the cemetery and had probably been made by the people who had lived in Nine Open Arms before us. I shoved the cart through the gap, only realizing how deep the hedge was once I'd forced my way through. It was like a thick, swaying castle wall.

The new cemetery was no longer really new. It had been laid out in 1905 because the old cemetery in the center of town was full. This cemetery, where Opa Pei was buried, was also beginning to fill up now. The town end was the most crowded, but here at our end, only a few plots were occupied. These were marked by simple gravestones that were barely weathered and not yet overgrown with moss. The only tombstone that looked somewhat older was the one closest to the hedge. This tomb didn't have an upright stone, but a knee-high flat slab overgrown with ivy.

I pumped the water. The screech of the handle cut to the bone.

When I returned, Dad and our brothers were busy making a separate entrance to the cigar workshop. Our brothers stood staring at the window that was going to become a door. Piet had drawn the outline with chalk. Dad shouted "excellent" before he had even had a look, but our brothers didn't take that as a sign that they were done. They calculated the angles to two decimal places, sketched, erased, and started over again, as if changing a window into a door was a matter of life and death.

That evening, Muulke was already sitting by the crack in the floor when Jess and I came into the bedroom. She had wrapped her coat around her like a cape and had a woolen cap on.

"This evening," she said.

"I don't think so," said Jess.

"We'll wait until they've gone to sleep again," said Muulke, without paying any attention to her.

"Tonight I'm staying in our wonderful warm bed," I said.

"Oh, shut up!" Muulke whispered loudly, but Jess and I didn't take any notice.

"Come on, quick," I said, pulling on my nightgown, shivering. "If you wait up, it will take even longer for the bed to warm up."

"Couldn't care less," Muulke hissed.

"Why is she staying out there?" said Jess as we crawled under the ice-cold blankets.

"She probably thinks Oma is going to tell another story about this house," I said.

"I'd rather have a story from the Crocodile," said Jess.

The Crocodile was Oma's large ancient suitcase. It was covered with linen, its corners were reinforced with reddish-brown metal caps, and it had a handle of cracked green leather—crocodile skin, Muulke knew for sure.

On good days, Oma Mei would produce photos from the Crocodile. They were carefully packed in various cloth-covered compartments with zippers and buttons. She would put a photo on the little silver tray that was also packed in the suitcase. We were allowed to touch the tray, but never the photos. Her stories were always about our grandfather or our mother.

"Ask about the time Opa Pei came home with three goats," she would say, for instance. "Ask what those blasted animals did to Monday's laundry." And she would tell the story of the farmer who had paid Opa Pei in kind for some work he had done on a new shed, and how she had gone to bring in the laundry, only to find three chewing goats and no laundry.

We didn't know how many photos were inside the Crocodile. For some of the photos there was more than one story, but asking anything about this was strictly forbidden. If we did, Oma Mei was likely to shut the case firmly, and her mouth, too. So we had learned to be quiet and to wait, no matter how much we wanted a story.

The day Oma Mei decided to unpack the Crocodile and display the photos would be the day we were going to stay somewhere. For good.

"We'll have a story tomorrow," I whispered.

"Do you think so?" Jess rolled onto her side.

"Lie straight."

Obediently, she turned onto her back again. I tickled her nose.

"Not all mothers have a heart as soft as a rag doll, do they?" Jess asked softly.

"Only very rare mothers," I said.

"How rare was ours?"

"As rare as a wreckbone."

I heard Muulke shifting. One of the buttons of her coat ticked against the floor. She scratched under her woolen cap. I wondered how long she would last. Jess shook me by the arm.

"Tell me."

"What?"

"A Crocodile story."

"Go to sleep now. Muulke?"

"Just an-nother m-minute," Muulke said stubbornly, her teeth chattering. "It'll s-start any m-minute now, I'll b-bet"

But Oma Mei made coffee and the clock ticked away, as Dad and our brothers played cards.

That was all.

"Tomorrow," said Muulke when she crawled into bed next

to us.

"Tomorrow," said Jess, and from her voice I could hear she was smiling.

We lay still and listened. Nine Open Arms told stories, too. When the wind blew, the tiles on the roof chattered, and when the wind blew from the east, the windows whistled in their frames. But on still evenings like this, there was plenty to hear from the house.

Some of the sounds were hard to recognize. Sometimes the house would say, "Frr-Frr." Or it hummed, with a high, far-off sound.

Disasters

THE FIRST DISASTER HAPPENED two days later.

Muulke, Jess, and I were getting the laundry from the line in the attic when suddenly the sunlight dimmed. We leaned on the ledge of one of the dormer windows and looked out.

"*Miljaar*!" said Jess.

From the east, above the undulating horizon of empty cornfields, pitch-black clouds were approaching. Between the earth and the sky, a dense, glowing curtain was moving.

"Here comes the rain the summer held back," Muulke said dreamily. "Now it's coming to make up for it all."

When the rain started, it sounded as if apples were falling on the roof.

"Muulke?" Oma Mei called from the bottom of the stairs. "Muulke?"

"I'm not doing anything," Muulke called back indignantly. "It's the house!"

We heard the storm pass over us, like a large, clumsy animal lifting itself over the roof with great difficulty. One moment, the panes in the dormer were dusty; the next I saw the rain beat off all the dirt and wash the glass clean. Then the roof started to leak. No, not to leak. It suddenly was as if we had no roof at all. That's how fast the water streamed in.

Our brothers stormed up the stairs, then came Dad, and finally Oma Mei, carrying the gray umbrella.

"Fing, Jess, Muulke, over here."

We stood under the umbrella while the rain pelted down.

"We're on it! We've got it!" shouted our brothers.

"Shouldn't we…" I started.

"And have you all in bed with pneumonia?" said Oma Mei. "Not on my life. Boys aren't girls, and girls aren't boys."

We watched our dad and brothers trying to take control. They fired off contradictory instructions at each other, and meanwhile the water poured in by the bucketful, until Oma Mei intervened. "Fing, rags and buckets from the kitchen cupboard. Muulke, pots and pans."

"And me? And me?" Jess asked eagerly.

"You keep an eye on everything," said Oma Mei. "Hurry up, Muulke and Fing."

Even though we caught some water here and there, it really was a hopeless job, for it turned out that the house leaked like a sieve. Water poured in everywhere, soaking Dad's and our brothers' hair and shoulders and turning their white shirts transparent. I could see their undershirts and their bony shoulders. Wet, they looked even more alike than dry.

It rained for all of ten minutes. Not much of a shower, really, but it created terrible havoc. It was as if a giant hand had picked up the house, dragged it through the River Meuse, and slammed it back down again on Sjlammbams Sahara.

The east side of the house was hit the worst. Along with the attic, our brothers' bedroom had begun to leak, too. Krit's and Sjeer's straw mattresses were soaked through. But that wasn't the worst of it.

Our brothers said it was so bad because it hadn't rained for such a long time. This had made the soil so hard that the water couldn't drain away except through its somewhat softened top layer. So the rain had streamed into the house, flooding the cellar through its small, unglazed windows. In the storeroom, the potatoes were floating around in brown, muddy water. In the second cellar, the *sjlamm* had gotten wet and had oozed out everywhere, so now only the very top of the heap still stuck out above the pitch-black water.

We'd forgotten all about the tobacco.

The five soggy bales leaned limply against each other, like elderly men on a hot day.

But even that wasn't the worst of it.

Under Oma Mei's soaking-wet mattress, the Crocodile lay in a puddle of dirty water. When we pulled it out and lifted it up, gray water poured out of it. Inside, behind the green velvet, zippers, and buttons, behind everything we'd thought made it secure, the photos of our grandfather and our mother were curling up and sticking together.

More Disasters

OMA MEI DIDN'T SAY a word. Not even when we dragged Eet's sodden straw mattress downstairs and it got hooked on a nail, leaving a trail of half-drowned hemp and straw all the way down the stairs. All she did was blink with her good eye, as if she was giving every bit of damage a secret mark and storing it in her head.

Dad, who was used to a constant stream of reproaches, found it hard to cope with her silence, so he escaped to the café, and our brothers quickly followed.

Muulke, Jess, Oma Mei, and I were in the living room, where the stove was burning with full force. We spread the potatoes and onions out on the floor and wrapped the briquettes of *sjlamm* in old newspapers. We hung the wet rags, blankets, and sheets over every door, chair, and table. Plaster had already started to crumble down from the ceiling. In one spot in the living room the wallpaper had started to come loose and behind it a crack had appeared in the wall.

"This is going to end badly," Muulke whispered later that evening.

Oma Mei lay on a borrowed straw mattress in the corner of our room. She was going to sleep with us until her room was usable again. Next to her, the Crocodile leaned on its open lid, with its zippers undone and straps loosened. We didn't know what had become of the photos. When Muulke asked, all she got from Oma was a snarl.

"This is going to end badly," Muulke said once more.

On the day we went to Mr. Walraven's shop to get wallpaper, we'd shouted, "unpack, unpack." But now that the photos were out of the suitcase at last, we no longer knew if this was what we wanted.

It took two weeks for Nine Open Arms to get back to normal, more or less.

We had the stove burning from early in the morning till late at night. It was stiflingly hot, but nobody dared complain.

The third cellar was the last part to be cleaned up. Making faces, Dad and our brothers brought everything upstairs: the stacks of soaked blankets covered in green mold, the mirror with its crumbling frame, the broken chairs, the bitter-smelling beer barrel. And the tombstone bed.

"See, now you're saying it yourself," said Muulke.

"Saying what?"

"You said, 'tombstone bed.'"

"I didn't."

"Did too."

"Did not."

"*Iepekriet.*"

"Blabbermouth."

"Liar."

"Softy."

"Nuisance."

"Bellyacher."

"Does it look like a tombstone?" Muulke asked Jess, but Jess didn't want to look.

"*Sjiethoes*," said Muulke. "Because it is so a tombstone."

"Then it's the first ever tombstone with legs," I said.

We didn't get much time to have a closer look. Oma Mei shooed us away and when we came back, everything was gone.

"Where's everything?" asked Muulke.

"That's none of your business," said Oma Mei, "but if you must know, it's gone to the dump and been burned."

Muulke cursed as soon as our grandmother was out of sight, but I didn't feel too sorry about it.

We weren't the only ones who had suffered from the rainstorm. In the center of the town, cellars were flooded and attics had sprung leaks. But our house seemed to be the only one where both things had happened.

All through the next week, it was as if Oompah Hatsi were back and had set up house not just in our street but throughout the town. Everywhere we went, from the market to the Putse Gate, we found pieces of furniture: plush chairs, lampshades, sideboards, even complete beds, all waiting for a ray of sunshine.

We hadn't known Sjlammbams Sahara had so many colors. The rain had revealed them all. With the dust now washed away, rocks and pebbles lay glittering in the sun. The earth revealed itself, too, and for a whole day it was not only reddish-brown and dark beige, but in the spots where the freshly washed grass grew, the soil had an almost purple glow.

At the end of November, it was winter for a week, and the hedge looked as if it had been sprinkled with caster sugar. It was a strange thing to see, a careless mixing of the seasons. But Sjlammbams Sahara made quick work of winter, since the snow disappeared the moment it touched the ground. Instead, a big puddle stretched along the cart ruts in the road, making it nearly impossible for us to reach the house without getting our feet wet. We had to walk right along the cemetery hedge, scraping against its dense greenery, to avoid the mud.

Meanwhile, Oma Mei and Dad were on speaking terms again, but something was obviously not quite right, and I knew it had to do with money. It was always about money, but now the problem seemed to be worse than ever before.

One afternoon, when we came home from school, the door that had once been a window (and now wasn't one or the other, just a hole with a board nailed across) stood open. Dad was sitting on a stool at the workbench. The rest of the room was still empty. Dad was wearing his best jacket, and a wilted carnation hung from his buttonhole.

"Tell me again about the opposite of worrying," I said.

He smiled. "Piet, Eet, Sjeer, and Krit have jobs."

"Oh," I said.

"Slaughtering." Smiling, he made a face. "For a short time. Until the tobacco permit gets here."

"When will it come?"

"Sometimes it can take a while."

"Can't you just start in the meantime?"

"If I got caught, I'd be fined. But there's no need. Piet, Eet, Sjeer, and Krit have jobs." He said it as if it was some sort of magic spell. "Perhaps I should..." He gave me a look.

I knew what I was supposed to say, but I didn't want to say it. I didn't want to have anything to do with those words, but they came anyway, of their own accord. "No, you don't need a job," I said. "The permit is coming. And then Krit, Sjeer, Eet, and Piet will come back, and you'll all make cigars. The best in town."

"Believe first, then see," said Dad.

"Exactly." I tried to laugh.

He looked at me again, but I couldn't bear the thought of more make-believe.

Muulke could, though. When I told her about Dad, she instantly invented a cigar factory that was famous all over the world, a town that was green with envy, and a cigar emperor who couldn't sell his cigars because of Dad's success. The emperor even went mad and took to drink.

"Dad's not going to go work at that slaughterhouse," she said. "He's been there already. That's why he's wearing his best jacket. They didn't want him."

"How do you know?"

"Don't ask why they didn't want him."

"I can guess," I said.

That evening, Muulke counted the disasters.

"One: the flood. Two: the permit that's not coming…"

"It always takes a while," I said. "Dad said so himself."

"Three: Oma Mei and Dad quarreling."

"Oma Mei is always quarreling. You know that as well as I do."

"And four—"

"Four nothing," I snapped.

She looked at me stubbornly. "Didn't I say so?"

"What?"

"That Nienevee has something to do with all of this."

"Did you say that?"

"This house is cursed."

"Oh, is it? First, you said it was a tragical tragedy."

Oma Mei came into the bedroom in her nightgown. She didn't have her nightcap on yet, and her gray hair stuck out in tangled tufts.

"Why aren't you in bed yet?" she wanted to know.

"We're waiting for Jess," said Muulke.

"You can wait lying down. Good night."

"Good night."

She slammed the door.

"I'm glad she's back in her own room," was Muulke's heartfelt response.

The house fell silent. For a while we stared at the Crocodile, which Oma Mei had left in our room, probably because she was afraid her own would leak again.

"That permit will be here within a week," I whispered. "I feel sure of it."

"Bet it won't."

"Bet it will."

But Muulke was right.

"It's the post office's fault," said the town hall.

"It's the town hall's fault," said the post office. "Try again next week."

"Things had better not get any worse," said Oma Mei. But they did.

The Curse of the Wandering Disk

IT HAPPENED ONE MORNING at recess.

Jess wanted to tie a loose shoelace. She bent forward and froze. I heard her gasp.

Nobody was allowed to touch her, not even me. The nuns gathered around, not knowing what to do.

But we did.

So we told them.

The nuns produced a bench from the gym, pushed it between Jess's legs, lifted her up carefully, and slowly, one small step at a time, walked into the building. She was like a statue being carried in a procession, but a twisted one. A Virgin Mary with a rigid, crooked back and shoulders pulled up high.

A wreckbone won't kill you, the doctors had said. (Not in those exact words, because they didn't call it a wreckbone, but one of those medical names nobody could or would remember.) Still, Jess did look as if she was dying. I'd never get used to it. It was horrible.

A circle formed around me and Muulke.

"What's the matter with her?" one of the girls asked.

"Nothing," Muulke said casually. "She's just twisted her back."

There were whispers, and I felt my face turn red.

"Come on, girls," said Sister Angelica. "Let's not turn this into a circus." And to me she said, "You'd better stay with her. The doctor will be here soon."

The nuns had pushed a desk up against the wall in the staff room. Jess was leaning against it. That way she didn't have to sit down, but still had support.

"I'm-fee-ling-bet-ter-now," said Jess. The pain cut her sentences into small slices. Her eyes were closed. Sweat stood out on her forehead. I held her hand. It felt cold and clammy.

"I-think-it's-get-ting-bet-ter."

I was silent. She opened her eyes.

"Now-the-whole-school-knows-a-bout-it."

"We've told them you just twisted your back."

"I'm-ug-ly," she said.

I could have slapped her. I wanted to scrunch her mouth shut. At the same time, I wanted to wrap my arms around her and never let her go.

"Shush," I said.

She was crying. Not loudly, not howling. Tears simply streamed down her face, and I suddenly saw that she was crying the way Oma Mei sometimes did after telling stories about our mother with her rag-doll heart.

When the doctor arrived, Jess changed back into her usual self. She moaned, she begged, she threatened, but there was nothing for it.

"It has to be done," I said, fighting back my own tears.

"It'll be over in no time," said the doctor. "Come, come, *kendj*. It isn't as bad as all that."

She had to lie on her stomach. I held her head.

"It's not fair," Jess cried. "Not fair."

The doctor pushed hard to get the bone back into the right place. I don't know which was worse, her scream or the soft whimpering that followed.

"And that makes five," said Muulke grimly when we heard Jess had to lie flat for a month. "Do you still believe we're just having a bit of bad luck?"

As soon as we got home, Oma Mei got busy with pillows, hot water bottles, extra blankets, tea in bed. She talked to Jess so softly that Muulke, on the other side of the door, could barely make out what she was saying.

"Muulke!" Suddenly, our grandmother was calling. "Seeing you're there anyway, could you possibly bring the Crocodile in here?" And when Muulke had brought in the suitcase, Oma Mei thanked her and asked her to kindly get lost.

Muulke and I went down to the garden. Our bedroom window stood open, so we could hear Oma Mei's voice, soft and lilting. Her Crocodile voice.

"Tea in bed, a hot water bottle, and a Crocodile story as well," Muulke said crossly. "It's not fair." She kicked a stone.

"You don't have a wreckbone."

"Sometimes I wish I did," Muulke grumbled.

"How can she still tell a Crocodile story?" I wondered aloud. "The photos aren't in the case, are they?"

"She must have hidden them under her apron."

"There are at least a hundred of them. They'd never fit."

"Well then, I've no idea where she put them," said Muulke.

Dad came around the corner. "Well?"

"Jess is getting better. The doctor pushed her wreckbone back in place."

Above us, Oma Mei talked on, though not loudly enough for us to understand anything. The three of us looked up.

"It's the story about the goat and the laundry line," said Muulke.

"How do you know?" asked Dad.

She shrugged.

"Come on," I said. "We have potatoes to peel."

Dad stayed where he was. He leaned against the wall and listened.

When we went into our bedroom that evening, the Crocodile was gone.

We looked under the bed and in the wardrobe. Then we sneaked into Oma Mei's room to search for it, after which we went into Dad's and our brothers' rooms. But we found no trace of it.

The suitcase seemed to have disappeared into thin air.

Hibernation

OUR GRANDMOTHER NO LONGER said, "Things had better not get any worse." Dad no longer mentioned "fresh air, as much as you want" or "living in a winter wonderland."

They carefully avoided each other.

Winter had arrived. Each morning, Muulke and I shuffled to school in the dark, pulling Jess behind us on the sled. ("No running, and stay together!")

On a bad day, the snow blew in great gusts over Sjlammbams Sahara and crept inside our clothes, no matter how carefully we wrapped ourselves up. Apart from the stretch where it went through the pass, the road to school had become invisible. The hedge along the cemetery guided us, but I still was relieved every time we saw the Putse Gate.

On the way home each afternoon, I felt confused when I saw the snow-covered roof of Nine Open Arms looming up behind the bare trees. On the one hand, the house felt unwelcoming, with its back turned toward us. On the other, it was where we lived and where Oma Mei waited for us, with hot tea, buttered bread sprinkled with sugar as a treat, and the crackling potbelly stove.

"Faster! Faster!" Jess shouted when we got to the hollow in the road.

"Mind her b—" I tried to warn, but Muulke was already racing ahead, pulling the sled behind her in wild jolts.

The permit still hadn't arrived.

"Sent two months ago," said the town hall.

"They're just saying that to get rid of you," said the post office.

"Back again?" said the town hall. "We're closed now."

"I'll put in a new application," said Dad.

"Your file will get confused," said the town hall.

Near the end of December, a thaw set in unexpectedly. On Christmas Day, we paraded around in our new dresses. They weren't really new. That was nothing unusual, since most children wore hand-me-down clothes. But Oma Mei didn't think that was good enough for her granddaughters, so at least once a year she got out our dresses and unstitched them. For three weeks, the table became a battlefield of sleeves, bodices, buttons, collars, ribbons, and trim. She kept sorting and arranging those bits and pieces until yet another new dress appeared.

Our Sunday dresses were, to put it mildly, something special. Oma Mei wasn't a skilled seamstress and sometimes she went a bit overboard in her efforts to make each dress look different. This year, for instance, there was a dress with a lace collar and three brass buttons. Another had short, puffy, acid-green shoulder caps from which long, checked sleeves emerged; and there was a tartan dress with a sailor collar. But we didn't say a word. We knew better than that.

Later that day, the whole family walked to church, carrying our Sunday shoes in paper bags. We slipped and slid in our summer shoes, which were already soaking wet from the half-thawed mud. When we were changing our shoes at the Putse Gate, a car passed us, moving at walking pace. In it, I saw a man smoking a gigantic cigar. Next to him, tall and straight, sat a woman in a fur coat. Piet, Eet, Sjeer, and Krit whistled softly. Dad raised his hand. The people in the car nodded.

"Who was that?" asked Muulke once the car had passed.

"The cigar emperor," said Sjeer.

"Next year, we'll ride in a car like that," said Dad.

"A bicycle would be nice," Oma Mei said grimly.

Christmas wasn't the only reason we were dressed in our Sunday best. December twenty-fifth was also the anniversary of Opa Pei's death. He had died a long time ago, even Dad had never known him. He had passed away before our father had even met our mother. We only knew him from the photos in the Crocodile, but when his name was read out in the commemoration of the dead during the Mass, Muulke, Jess, and I felt excited and solemn at the same time.

"Yes, yes, Pei was quite a character," the old women and men would say every year after the Mass. They looked as if they could tell some good stories, but Oma Mei never gave them the chance. She would sweep us out of the church, waving to the left and greeting to the right, without ever stopping. Even the parish priest had to be content with a wave that looked more like a slap than a greeting.

After Mass that Christmas Day, we laid a wreath, made of branches from the hedge along the new cemetery, on our grandfather's grave. It was an ordinary grave—an upright gray stone with a rounded top and a gray stone slab with plain letters and numbers.

PETRUS JOHANNES MARIE TRUI KLEIN
APRIL 6, 1861–DECEMBER 25, 1918

It always made us a bit nervous to be there. Not because we were at our grandfather's grave, but because his name wasn't the only one on the gravestone. Next to it was carved:

MARIA HUBERTINA CAROLA VICTORINA KLEIN-WALRAVEN
DECEMBER 9, 1875–

Even though Dad had explained at least a hundred times that it was quite normal for married couples to select a grave together, it still made us nervous to see our grandmother's name there—particularly because of that tiny dash between life and death.

As soon as we got home, we changed out of our Sunday dresses, while our brothers made hot chocolate. Dad played *Silent Night, Holy Night* on his mouth organ, and, for a little while, everything seemed good. And then, things even got a little better.

"Ask," said Oma Mei, who was sitting by the potbelly stove with cheeks as red as apples. "Ask who, as a young girl, was chosen to sing the solo at midnight Mass. Ask who practiced so long and so hard that on that very night her voice was as hoarse as a crow's."

The Crocodile appeared from under the sofa. "Is that where it was?" said Muulke, sounding utterly surprised.

From outside, the Crocodile looked more discolored and cracked than ever. The locks were so rusty it no longer even closed properly, and the inner lining, with all its zippers and buttons, had been taken out. But the photos were back, lying on the hard dented cardboard.

"Poor dear Crocodile," said Jess, full of pity.

"Is anybody going to ask the next question?" said Oma Mei. Picking up the silver tray, she carefully brought out a small battered photograph of our young mother in a stylish dress, a big shawl around her neck.

At the end of February, everything froze over, and after that there were terrible storms. At carnival time, the two apple trees at the back of our garden were blown over, making a noise like that of a china cabinet collapsing. Eet and Krit, dressed up as Harlequins in costumes they'd borrowed from the butcher, went to inspect the damage but didn't get very far. The wind was so strong they were literally blown back into the house.

From March on, though, the weather improved. There was a lot of rain, but because we now knew where the worst holes were, the damage wasn't too bad. At the first sign of rain, we'd run up the stairs ("Don't run! Don't run!") and place buckets, pots, and cups over the attic floor, until the day when Nol brought a load of roof tiles that he "just happened to have lying around." His tiles were orange, the ones on our roof black, so from a distance the roof now looked like the wings of a molting bird. The paint on the windowsills had flaked off some more and the wood under it was split and crumbling, but at least the cellar windows had been nailed shut to prevent the cellar from flooding again.

And then, finally, when we'd almost forgotten it was possible, spring arrived.

And with the spring, new mysteries.

The Opposite of Worrying [2]

———————

I WAS PUMPING. THE pump-handle gave a heart-stopping screech and the water poured into the tubs, where it glittered like magic dust.

I felt more and more comfortable in the graveyard. Nine Open Arms was bigger than any other house we had ever lived in, and our brothers were away more and more often, yet the house still seemed to be bursting with voices, quarrels, footsteps, squeaking doors, creaking windows, and feet stomping up and down the stairs. And even though we'd never had a room to ourselves before, when Muulke and Jess were bickering once again for the millionth time, I had the feeling that I was stuck in that room—stuck in the whole, entire house, really.

But the graveyard was my own. There were visitors, of course, but they usually stayed near the grave they were visiting, as if it was a fire that would keep them warm. And funerals were always between nine and four. So in the hours before and after, the cemetery was my own. When I stood behind the hedge it was, for a moment, as if Nine Open Arms and my family no longer existed.

When the two tubs were full, I was surprised to notice that someone had cleaned the old grave—the grave that had only a flat slab. The ivy had been removed. Now I could see that the grave was made of weathered black marble. A large, deep crack ran straight across the stone. I could smell a vague scent of soft soap.

There was no name on the grave and no date.

"Fing! Fing!"

The hedge shook and Muulke shot through the gap. She didn't have shoes on and her socks were covered in mud. She didn't have a coat on, either.

"What's happened?" I asked.

But she only signaled for me to come, turned around, and disappeared through the shaking hedge.

As I ran after Muulke, my head was full of the most horrible images. I saw Dad hit on the head by a falling roof tile. Oma Mei slipping on the stairs. It couldn't be Jess again, could it?

They were standing around the kitchen table, murmuring. I quickly looked from one to the other. They were all there. My knees nearly gave way I was so relieved.

"What?" I asked. "What?"

Muulke and Jess made room for me. I couldn't see anything, just the table, until Muulke pointed.

On the table lay something that at first seemed insignificant: small and creased, it was an envelope, covered with stamps and postmarks, faded and illegible.

I held my breath when I realized what I was looking at. "Is that…?"

Dad nodded. Nobody said anything. As if a single word would make the letter disappear again.

"As if it couldn't find us!" Muulke exclaimed. "As if it had to wander all over the world before finding us."

The day after the permit had finally found us, the opposite of worrying arrived for a second time.

"It's the third picking, so it's not the finest quality tobacco," said Nol. "No, I don't want anything for it. No ifs and buts, Antoon. I am doing it for those kids and their mother. God rest her soul."

Oma Mei cried. They weren't tears of sorrow, nor tears of joy, more something in between. The men, including our brothers, carried on as if they were busy with something that needed lots of noise and cursing. Especially Nol.

"Now listen," said Oma Mei later. "There's a very busy time ahead. That workshop has to be finished. So don't get under your father's and your brothers' feet."

"No, Oma Mei."

"I am going to help Nol's wife, Nettie. She's having another baby, and it's the least I can do."

"Yes, Oma Mei."

"And wipe that grin off your face, Muulke. If you think you're going to be in the promised land here, you're mistaken."

She gave each of us a list.

"My list is much longer than Jess's," Muulke complained.

"Swap?" Jess said instantly.

"No swapping," said Oma Mei.

I looked at their lists. They weren't half as long as mine.

"If I leave it to those two, it's going to be a mess," said Oma Mei. "You know that."

I didn't say a word.

It was a real upheaval. In the morning, our grandmother set the table, but she left for Nol and Nettie's house before we'd even had breakfast.

I helped Jess into her straightener. I tightened the straps. The slats on either side of her spine pressed into her flesh. I immediately heard her breathing become shallower.

"Oma Mei never makes them so tight," Jess complained.
I bit my lip and thought of my list.

"STRAIGHTENER JESS," it said. "THIRD HOLE." And below that, the proof that our grandmother knew us better than anyone else: "FING, DON'T BELIEVE HER IF SHE SAYS IT SHOULD BE LESS TIGHT."

Downstairs, our brothers were loudly listing all the things that had to be done. The door between the living room and the workshop had to be sealed. Two new worktables and four chairs had to be built. The presses oiled, the molds waxed, walls painted, a heater installed. No *ulezeik*, that was for sure.

Muulke shouted that their voices had become a mile deeper in a week. Of course she was exaggerating, but I was also aware that something had changed. It was as if that letter had dragged Nine Open Arms out of its hibernation, straight into the demands and responsibilities of the real, grown-up world. And it had pulled us along, too.

"Now we'll have to tell ourselves not to run," said Muulke on our way to school. "Now we'll have to cuff our own ears if we get our shoes dirty or tear our clothes." She grinned.

"Keep walking," I said.

"Yes, Oma Mei," said Muulke.

"Or we'll be late."

"Not if you're with us," said Muulke.

"Do you have the dough?" I asked.

"Dough?"

"For the baker, you idiot."

Muulke stared at me stupidly. I sighed.

"Oma left it out ready in the kitchen. In those two towels."

We didn't bake our own bread. Dad had promised to build a brick oven, but he hadn't gotten around to it yet. So Oma Mei kneaded the dough and took it to the bakery to be baked. That was cheaper than buying bread.

"*Miljaar*!" Muulke shouted and turned around.

"You'll be late," I warned. "Forget it."

But Muulke would rather face the nuns' wrath than Oma Mei's. She raced off. I heard her footsteps fading in the distance.

Jess shuffled along behind me.

"What's the matter?" I asked.

"Nothing."

"Muulke will be back in a minute."

We emerged from the pass and the wind hit us in the face.

"I want to go back to our old school," Jess said. "I want to go back to our old house."

"Can't be done," I said. "Keep moving."

A few girls were standing around on the corner where we usually stopped to catch our breath. I didn't really know them, but I knew enough to know it wouldn't be wise to pick a fight with them. They came from a part of the city we knew to stay away from.

"Do you want anything?" they said as we passed by.

"Don't say anything," I told Jess.

"Not answering?" One of them grabbed me by my sleeve. She was the only one I knew by name: Fat Tonnie. The story was that she had been attacked by a rabid dog once and had bashed the animal to death with a hammer. She was much older than the others in the group; she'd had to repeat a year twice already. I had heard that the nuns only let her move up to get rid of her.

The group blocked our way.

"Aren't you from outside the walls?" asked one of the girls.

"We have to go," I said.

"I don't think so," said Fat Tonnie with a grin.

"They stink," said another girl. "Everything from outside the walls stinks."

They started to surround us, and I don't know what would have happened if Muulke hadn't come panting around the corner right then. She looked Fat Tonnie up and down with her Sergeant Major's look and Fat Tonnie looked her up and down. An icy silence fell.

Then Muulke said calmly, "Come on, it's late."

"Very late," said Fat Tonnie.

She didn't actually let go of my sleeve, but I was able to yank myself from her grip without too much trouble.

When I walked into the schoolyard in the mornings now, I no longer felt sick. The girls in my class waved or said hello. Sometimes they even chatted with me or I joined them at jump rope. But I still had no friends. I told myself it was because the other girls had known each other for such a long time. But when I watched Muulke, who had a crowd following her every recess, I knew that wasn't the whole truth. And I felt a stab of jealousy.

A Table Full of
Better-Luck-Next-Time Cigars

"OF COURSE, YOU DON'T become a cigar emperor just like that," said Dad.

It was evening. We had eaten, cleared the table, and were halfway through the washing up, when Sjeer came into the kitchen and announced they had a surprise.

"That's sure to be something special," Oma Mei said scornfully, but she came along anyway.

The table in the workshop was covered with tobacco leaves, fillers, knives, molds, and in the center lay the better-luck-next-time cigars. Some had split outer leaves, Dad explained, because they had been packed too tightly. Then there were some that were floppy because they hadn't been packed tightly enough. And there were dud cigars that only looked all right from the outside.

Piet, Eet, Sjeer, and Krit swept them all up, and then put them down again one by one.

"Filler's too soft," said Dad giving one cigar a little squeeze. "This one will burn up faster than newspaper. And this one here is too hard." He solemnly put the cigar into his mouth and held a match to it, but the thing would barely catch fire. "A stone would burn more easily," he said, holding the cigar between his teeth.

Suddenly, Jess burst into tears. Everybody looked up. Oma Mei gathered her on to her lap.

"What's the matter, little one?"

"Now it i-is n-never going to h-happen again."

"What, *leeveke*?"

Jess said something, but nobody could understand her.

"What?"

Jess tried to control her heaving. Her nose was running.

"The op-p-p-osite of w-worrying."

"Where did you get that idea?"

Jess's shoulders shook. Her voice cracked.

"Everything g-goes wr-rong. Everything goes wrong all the time."

I heard Oma Mei take a deep breath.

"No, not really," Dad began, but then he fell silent. I could feel my feet tensing up inside my shoes. The silence dragged on.

"That's exactly the idea," Oma Mei finally said. "Better-luck-next-time cigars have to go wrong to begin with so your brothers can learn what not to do. After that, they'll make... um...good-luck cigars. Isn't that how it works, Antoon? First better-luck-next-time cigars, then good-luck cigars? Isn't that right?"

Dad cleared his throat and stared at the ceiling before finding his voice again. "Exactly. How...um...do you think... Nol started off? Or Leon Kamps in Station Street? Or Filip Mols, the cigar emperor? Do you think they got everything right the first time? No, no, of course not. Of course they didn't."

Dad followed that up with the usual stuff about first believing and then seeing, and the opposite of worrying. We groaned and fumed, but deep inside we were relieved. It felt as if we had just escaped a major disaster by the skin of our teeth.

Eet brought in the cherries in brandy. "To celebrate."

But Oma Mei resolutely shook her head. "There will be something to celebrate when you've sold the first cigar." She put the blue jar way up on the top shelf. We toasted with orange cordial instead.

"Here's to the good-luck cigars!" our brothers shouted.

"Here's to the opposite of worrying," shouted Dad.

Oma Mei didn't join in, but when we asked for the Crocodile she didn't object. "Ask me about the time Opa Pei had a wall built for an elephant," she said.

It was a story about our grandfather, soon after he had become a supervisor. Oma Mei and he had just recently moved into a new house. There were a few things still to be done, but because he was so busy he had instructed his bricklayers to build a small wall in the kitchen.

"Are you sure that thing is solid?" Oma Mei had asked suspiciously.

And Opa Pei had replied, "My dear, even an elephant can safely lean against it!"

But the following evening, when he started hammering a nail into the wall to hang up their wedding picture, the wall started to sag like melting butter, and then, with a huge roar, it crumbled.

We peered at the photo. It didn't really go with the story because Opa Pei was clearly too old, but there weren't many good pictures of him. For this one, he had posed properly. There were a number of men in the photo, and Opa Pei stood in front. His eyes were shining, he grinned from ear to ear, and he wore an expensive felt hat and a silk vest. Behind him stood his bricklayers in their shabby shirts and caps. One of them seemed to be laughing uproariously.

"Why is that man laughing so hard?" asked Muulke.

Jess and I nudged her furiously.

"Of course, those bricklayers were in big trouble," Oma Mei said after a few icy seconds. "And they had to rebuild the wall immediately, even though it was Sunday. Because it wasn't all right for a supervisor's wife to have a collapsed wall. Yes, that's what your grandfather was like."

Later that evening, when we were in bed, we discovered why Jess had burst into tears.

"The Crocodile is back in her bedroom," Jess said. "I've seen it with my own eyes."

"I can't see what's so terrible about that," said Muulke. "It's been there before."

"Yes, but it was always under her bed."

"Isn't it under her bed anymore?"

Jess shook her head. "No, *iepekriet*. It's standing right next to her bed. On its side."

Muulke was too upset to tease Jess back. "*Miljaar!*" was all she could muster.

If anyone could sense another move in the air, it was Oma Mei. And we in turn could tell from where the Crocodile stood just how much longer we were going to remain somewhere.

"Next to her bed," said Muulke. "Then it will be another month at the most."

Jess shivered. "But that isn't all. The cover is on it already."

Muulke looked scared. "Three weeks at the most then."

"Stop it now," I said. They glared at me. I took a deep breath.

"You know as well as I do that she is terrified that the house will start leaking again, so she'd hardly put the Crocodile under her bed, would she?"

"But—"

"It's much safer on its side, can't you see that?" I interrupted. "And with the cover around it, it's even more protected. And Oma Mei would not have agreed with Dad about the opposite of worrying if she thought that everything was going to go wrong again, would she?"

I could feel Muulke and Jess exhale. "You're just a pair of *sjiethoezer*," I said.

"*Iepekriet*," said Jess, with a sigh of relief.

I turned over, felt Jess's left foot sliding over mine, and I knew that with her right foot she was trying to find Muulke.

"So you believe that the opposite of worrying is here to stay?" said Jess, snuggling into the crook of my arm.

"Yes."

"Then I believe my wreckbone will get cured."

"Shush," I said.

"And that everything is going to be all right."

"Absolutely."

"Everything."

"Shush."

"Believing first, then seeing."

"Go to sleep now."

"Do you remember 'Nine Open Arms'?"

"Sleep."

"That name was because of me, wasn't it?"

"Absolutely because of you, but now close your eyes."

Muulke was the first to fall asleep, but it took quite a while for Jess to fall off. I twisted and turned. What if Jess was right? What if the opposite of worrying was never going to arrive? What if before long we had to move once more? Pack up all our things, move to a new place, and start all over again?

"Moving is letting your story start afresh," Dad had said one day. But I didn't need a new story. Not that Nine Open Arms was the house of my dreams. But sometimes just staying somewhere was good enough.

It took me a long time to fall asleep.

More Riddles

IT WAS MIDDAY. THE laundry had been boiled and put out to bleach. The bed sheets and the tablecloth were hanging over the fence to dry in the spring sunshine. We were just finishing with the last of the wash when they came out.

"Gone," said Sjeer.

"Vamoosed," said Eet.

"Vanished," said Piet.

"No, stolen," said Krit.

It must have happened while they were having coffee in the kitchen. Our brothers had left the workshop door open, and when they'd returned, the cigars were gone.

"Twelve of them," said Sjeer. "We'd made fifty and now there are only thirty-eight left."

We all looked at Dad, who stood with our brothers, but hadn't said anything yet. He chewed the inside of his cheek thoughtfully.

Then he said briskly, "At least someone thinks they're worth stealing."

Oma Mei said nothing. She didn't blame Dad for leaving

the door that used to be a window standing open. She didn't even make a snide remark about bad cigars that probably nobody would want anyway. But that evening when Jess was too scared to go upstairs after Muulke had said the cigar thief was hiding under our bed, she let us have it.

"Just think for a second and stop being such a *sjiethoes* for once," she snapped at Jess. "How big do you think that cigar snatcher can be if he fits under your bed? There's hardly enough room for a cigar."

She was probably shocked by her own outburst, because she went upstairs with Jess after and looked under the bed. And when Jess was still uneasy, she fetched a broom and poked around under it some more.

"There you are, now he's dead as a dodo," she said. "And now it's time for you to undress and get into bed."

The next day, on our way home from school, we saw a man riding a bicycle down Sjlammbams Sahara ahead of us. At least, he was trying to ride his bike, but the wind was so strong and there were so many potholes and muddy puddles that he constantly had to stop and get off. Sometimes we lost sight of him for a bit, but then he'd show up again at the end of a curve, or on top of a rise.

"Where's he heading?" Muulke wondered.

"Perhaps he's a customer," Jess said.

"A customer?"

"Someone who wants to buy our cigars."

We looked at each other.

"Come on," said Muulke, and she took off at a run.

"Not so fast," Jess puffed. And before we even got to the next bend she stopped, gasping for breath, furious. "Wait! Wait!"

The man was standing at our gate when Muulke and I arrived. His bicycle, which he'd leaned against the fence, was covered in mud and the cuffs of his trousers were stained. His thin hair was stuck to his forehead.

"Is your father at home?"

He didn't look at us. Instead, he stared at the door that used to be a window. We could clearly hear Dad inside, cursing the press.

"Have you come for cigars?" I asked, still huffing and puffing.

"They have a really good flavor," Muulke panted. "And they're nice and spicy," she added. I gaped at her, wondering where she'd found those words.

The man was still staring at the workshop where Dad was obviously giving the press a kick, for we heard a muffled thump followed by a string of very clear swear words.

"Hello?" the man called, without much conviction. He looked at the muddy puddle between the gate and Nine Open Arms and then at his shoes again. They were patent leather shoes with black laces. He opened his flat briefcase and produced a bright-white, perfectly crisp envelope.

"Will you give him this, please?" he requested. He blushed as he spoke, which made me blush, too. I nodded and accepted the letter. Then he grabbed his bike, obviously relieved, and started on his way back, his heels on the pedals.

"Don't forget!" he called.

"What's that?" Muulke wanted to know when he had disappeared around the first bend.

"A letter," I said.

"Yes, even my nose can see that. What sort of letter?"

"How should I know?" I held the envelope with both hands. The folds were sharp as knives. A severe white letter.

"The Rotterdam Banking Society," Muulke read. "Isn't that Dad's bank? Why would the bank send him a letter?" She looked worried. "It must be about money. Open it."

"Are you out of your mind?"

"What do you want to do, then? Wait until the Crocodile leaves of its own accord?"

"Yes, but—"

"Give it to me!"

"No!"

"Fine. So don't." She shrugged, as if she didn't care, but the moment my attention wandered, she snatched the letter.

"Let go," I hissed.

"You let go."

"Muulke, let go!"

Then the inevitable happened: with a dismal sound the letter tore in half. Horrified, we stared at the two pieces.

Things happened very fast after that. Jess came around the bend, her eyes angry and full of tears. At the same moment, the workshop door opened and Dad came out. I must have panicked, but it was a strange kind of panic, because while my heart was hammering in my chest and I could feel myself blushing, my hands were calm. I snatched the other half of the letter from Muulke, tore the whole thing into tiny pieces, and threw the whole handful toward the cemetery hedge, where the wind carried them away.

Muulke stared at me with a look of horror and admiration on her face.

There was a full moon that night. Jess lay on her back, frowning in her sleep. Muulke was on her side with one leg forward and the other back, as if she was running. I twisted and turned, so much that it was a small miracle that neither of my sisters woke up.

What in the world had I done? What if someone found out? An important letter like that couldn't just disappear. But had it actually been an important letter? Was it a letter about money? More debts? Could it be something else? But what?

There was only one thing to do.

I slipped quietly out of bed, put on my dress and sweater, grabbed my socks, and walked quietly out of the room and down the passage. Moonlight shone through the window on to the landing, drawing a straight track over the uneven floor. For a moment, I stood by the dark stairwell, listening.

Through the bedroom doors, all slightly ajar, I could hear snoring and breathing. I waited, counting to ten, till I was sure no one had woken up. Then I went downstairs. Everything would have come off perfectly if my mind hadn't been preoccupied with the letter. It made me forget about the sixth step. Putting my full weight on it, I felt it sink under me, as I heard its wailing tear the silence apart. For minutes that felt like hours, I stood stock-still. I was convinced that Oma Mei had heard me and that she was about to come storming on to the landing, her swivel-eye spinning in alarm.

But nothing happened.

Downstairs, the table was already set for breakfast. The moonlight was so clear I could even see the pale green edges of the breakfast plates. The cutlery gleamed, and cutting through that strange silence came the ticking of the clock.

The kitchen door wasn't locked.

Outside, the wind had dropped. The sky was clear, apart from a few wisps of haze. Like a huge dented egg, the moon hung high above Sjlammbams Sahara. Carefully avoiding the muddy puddle in front of our house, I walked to the gate. Here, too, it was remarkably quiet, as if a giant blanket covered the whole world.

I walked up to the garden wall, which seemed higher and more massive with every step I took.

I searched in the grass. I searched in the hedge. I searched along Sjlammbams Sahara as far as the pass. After five minutes, my shoes and dress were soaked through, and even though it wasn't a very cold night, I was shivering. Step by step, my feeling of hopelessness grew. Had I really thought I would be able to find those snippets of paper on that windy road?

I stood with my back to Nine Open Arms and peered down Sjlammbams Sahara.

In the distance, I saw the familiar ink-black outline of the main church. Somewhere, a fox yipped.

I thought of Fie, asleep in the house opposite our old house. I thought about how we used to reach for each other with our hands through the window. And I thought of the time when Muulke had pushed a plank through the window to crawl across it to the other side, and how Oma Mei, as always, must have felt trouble looming and had come thundering into the room just as Muulke had put her knee on the ominously creaking plank.

I felt a great wave of homesickness come over me, a terrible homesickness, and I knew I would never be able to feel that way about Nine Open Arms, even if our next move really were to take us to the end of the earth. I don't cry often, but I felt tears coming, and I did nothing to hold them back. Nothing made any sense anymore. The whole thing made no sense. It wouldn't be long before they found out about the letter. Oma Mei would explode and Dad would try to smooth things over, which would only make Oma Mei more furious. Dad would walk out, stay away for a long time, and then he'd come back with a new plan, a new place to live, a new opposite of worrying. We had been through it all so many times before.

Suddenly, everything seemed completely hopeless.

I sobbed loudly, and with every howl some of the pressure that had built up in my head and my heart was released. I covered my face with my hands and felt terrible and relieved at the same time.

When, after a while, a wail that wasn't my own cut through my wailing, I thought in my misery that it must be the fox who was crying with me. But when I realized what I was hearing— what I was really hearing—my head cleared in an instant, and I turned in amazement. I knew the sound. I had heard it often enough before. What's more, I had made that sound myself. It was the pump in the cemetery. Someone was pumping water. In the dead of night, someone was busy pumping water!

Later, this would become one of our favorite what-if stories.

What if we'd come home from school later that day?

What if we'd missed the man from the Rotterdam Banking

Society and hadn't then fought about the letter?

Would I still have discovered what I discovered that night?

Would we ever have solved the mystery of Nine Open Arms?

If it had been a ghost, some remnant of Muulke's tragical tragedy, I wouldn't have found it all that strange. Perhaps I'd even been expecting something like that. But it was no ghost.

In the moonlight, among the looming white gravestones, pale as a ghost but with a grim expression that had nothing ghostly about it, and moving her arms in a vigorous way I'd have recognized anywhere, sat Oma Mei. She sat by the grave without a name and scrubbed and scoured as if her life depended on it.

They're Just Beds

DAD AND OUR BROTHERS had gone out. Oma Mei was still at Nol and Nettie's. And I was waiting to talk with Muulke without Jess around, since I didn't want to make her even more fearful than she already was.

The three of us were sitting on the wooden fence in front of the house.

"Will you do something for me?" I asked Jess.

I pointed at the baby carriage with the empty tubs inside.

"Me?"

"All you have to do is take the tubs to the cemetery and pump water into them. I'll bring the full tubs back."

She stared at me.

"Now's your chance," I said. "With Oma Mei still away…" I knew she loved doing jobs she wasn't supposed to do.

I watched Jess thinking. Her coal-black eyes became even darker. She was the only one of us who had eyes like that. She'd inherited them from our mother with the rag-doll heart.

"Only if you come with me."

I shook my head. "All or nothing."

"But my wreckbone…"

"It can handle it."

"But Oma Mei says…"

"Sometimes Oma Mei exaggerates."

Jess looked toward the cemetery. I could see her hesitating, and I could see that fear was winning out. I should have known better. No matter how much Jess wanted to be part of everything, she would always be scared of the cemetery.

Muulke shifted next to me. "If you half-shut your eyes," she said, "and look at the gravestones, they look just like beds. With headboards and footboards. So tell yourself, 'They're just beds.'"

Jess stared at the hedge.

"Say it," said Muulke.

"They're just beds…"

"And nothing else."

"And nothing else."

"Once more."

Jess repeated the words again and again. I was relieved to see her hunched shoulders relax a little. She took hold of the baby carriage. Muttering, her eyes already squinting shut, she walked over to the hedge. She turned around at the gap.

"Just beds," Muulke called.

"Only pumping," I warned. "I'm doing the rest."

Jess waved and was gone.

I told Muulke everything. At first, when I told her how I'd snuck outside by myself, she looked jealous. When I told her how I'd searched around on my knees for the snippets of paper, she laughed. But finally, when she had heard the rest, she fell silent.

"Oma Mei?"

"Yes."

"In the middle of the night in the cemetery?"

"Yes."

"And she was scrubbing the gravestone without a name?"

"As if it was a matter of life and death."

Muulke whistled. Then she said nothing for awhile, but I could see something brewing in her eyes. Suddenly, I wasn't sure telling her had been such a good idea.

"Strange things happen here," she said in a lugubrious voice.

"One strange thing," I said.

Muulke shook her head. "And what about those stolen cigars? And that 'Arghh!' from under the ground?"

Perhaps I'd been expecting that she'd give me a logical explanation. Or that she'd laugh at me. I would have preferred anything to what she was doing now.

"We heard that only once," I said. "And we haven't heard it since. And those cigars…they were just stolen. It happens all the time."

"And Oma Mei scrubbing gravestones in the middle of the night, does that happen all the time, too?"

"Maybe I dreamed it," I snapped.

"You wish!"

Sometimes I hated Muulke so much I scared myself.

"You can hit me later," Muulke said calmly. "But first you have to listen." She shifted, picked a bit at the splintery wood, and smoothed her dress.

"Perhaps Oma Mei walks in her sleep?" I tried. But who was I trying to fool?

"You're not the only one who's discovered something," said Muulke.

"What?"

In the distance the pump handle began to squeak.

"Do you remember the flood?"

"What about it?"

"When Dad and our brothers dragged everything from the third cellar?"

"Yes?"

Muulke was silent.

"Muulke." I was getting annoyed. "Stop being such a drama queen. Just tell me."

She jumped off the fence. "You'd better come and see for yourself."

"Quickly then," I said. "I want to be back before Jess has finished."

Mr. Wetsels' field was next to our house, bounded on one side by the fence on which we had been sitting. Near the fence stood a small shed, built of pieces of old timber with a roof of broken tiles. It had a small window on one side.

"Here," said Muulke. She lifted the shed door up from the bottom and shook it a few times. I heard a metallic click, and then the door slid open with hardly any noise.

I stopped at the threshold. "So?"

"At the back."

She shoved me suddenly and I stumbled inside. The floor was clay and weathered cement. A smell of sweat, old rags, and cow manure hung in the air.

"Are you crazy?" I complained. "I could have fallen. God knows what sort of creepy crawlies there are on this floor."

Muulke said nothing. When I turned, all I could see was her finger pointing to the half-dark corner.

It took a little while before I could see anything. I frowned.

"Well?" Muulke said triumphantly.

"Well what?"

What did she expect? That I'd faint? After wreckbone curses, floods, disappearing letters, and Oma Mei scrubbing a gravestone in the middle of the night, there wasn't all that much left that would shock me.

We stared at the old bed that leaned in pieces against the wall. I remembered the last time we had seen it, when the "Arghh!" came up from under the cellar floor. But there was nothing scary about it now. It was just a shabby piece of furniture that had been taken apart and put away. Nobody would ever sleep in it again. Rather than scary, it was sad. Without thinking about it, I took a step closer. The crumbled cement cracked under my feet.

"Awful, isn't it?" said Muulke.

I recognized the knobs on the headboard. Automatically, I stretched out my hand. The knobs felt strangely familiar. I slid my finger down along the carved wood.

"Leaves," Muulke said softly. "All the legs have leaves carved on them. Almost real, as if they're blowing around in the wind. Lovely, isn't it?"

"It's just a stupid old bed," I said, still smarting over her push.

And then it happened.

As if the sun was protesting my conclusion, a beam of light suddenly streamed through the little window. Countless dust motes floated by. I felt the warmth of the coming summer, and I heard Muulke take a deep breath, or perhaps it came from me?

Next to the bed's headboard stood its footboard. It was lower than the headboard and had graceful scrolls at the top. But what took my breath away was the picture before me.

Carved into the board was an exquisite landscape of fields full of waving corn, a town in the distance, and, in the middle, a long, winding road with…

"What's that?" asked Muulke, surprised.

"It looks like a little chair," I said.

We looked at the tiny carved chair sitting on the road.

"What's that chair doing in the middle of Sjlammbams Sahara?" we both exclaimed.

Because we'd instantly recognized our road and our town.

"Oma Mei knows more about this," Muulke said when we were outside again.

"Like what?"

"Something we don't know anything about."

"Yes, but what?"

"Stop it," said Muulke, annoyed. "I don't know yet. But I'll find out."

I sighed. "Just like last year when you said you'd find out what the matter was with Mrs. Brouwers?"

"That was something else altogether."

"You seemed to think she'd stolen her neighbor's earrings."

"It could have been true."

"Or that time when you followed Mattie from the fairground for a whole week?"

"He has hair on his back. You've seen it yourself."

"But that doesn't mean I immediately thought he was a werewolf."

Muulke shrugged. "Just because I was wrong once doesn't mean I'm wrong all the time. Oma Mei is behaving strangely, that's for sure. She scrubs gravestones in the middle of the night and says that she's burned the bed when all the while it's here."

"Perhaps she changed her mind."

"If that's so, then why did she say everything had been burned? And why does she hide it here instead of storing it in the cellar? And why—"

But I never found out what more she wanted to ask, because at that moment we heard a bloodcurdling scream.

As we ran up the road we saw Jess plunging through the gap in the hedge, sobbing. She stumbled across Sjlammbams Sahara. I ran toward her. She hurled herself at me so violently I nearly toppled over.

While I was trying to get my footing, she clung to me so hard that it felt like she wanted to climb up on me. Her hands gripped my arms like a little bird's claws.

"What's the matter this time?" Muulke asked.

Jess whimpered. I couldn't understand a word of what she was trying to say.

"Calm down. Ouch! Don't pinch! Jess! What's wrong?"

"Dea-dea-o-y!"

"What did you say?"

"A-dea-o-y!" She swallowed and bit her lip. "A dead body!"

"Where?"

"In the cememe… cemetery."

"That's where they belong," said Muulke dryly.

Jess's eyes flashed. Her face was twisted, as if the tears still wanted to come, but her anger was winning out.

"There was a dead body. A real one, Fing."

"Perhaps you thought you saw a real one," I said.

"It was real!" Jess screamed. She kicked the gate.

"Careful! Your back!" Muulke and I cried in unison.

Muulke and I walked through the cemetery, hand in hand.

"It's really true," Jess shouted from the other side of the hedge.

"So what did that body look like?" Muulke shouted back.

Silence.

Then, "I couldn't really see."

"You saw a body," I called, "but you couldn't see what it looked like?"

"I saw a part of it."

"A part?"

"An arm."

Muulke and I looked at each other.

"An arm?"

"Yes."

"Where?"

"Well, actually it wasn't an arm," shouted Jess. "More like a hand."

"A hand?"

"A finger. But it was horribly dead and it was sticking out of that little window."

"Window?"

"In the hedge."

Muulke tapped her forehead. At that moment, even I didn't know what to think. Windows, hands, bodies. One thing I did know was that sending Jess to the cemetery had been the dumbest thing I could ever have done.

"Fing," said Muulke.

"What?"

"Fing!"

"What?"

"Over there."

She pointed.

It was by now several months since the hedge had been trimmed, and although it was still very straight, its outline was softening a little.

Still, there was no question that a hole had been carved into the hedge.

No, it wasn't the untidy gap we always went through, but a definite hole right in the middle of the hedge. Or, no, not a hole. Jess was right. It was more like a little window. It was no larger than a handkerchief and if I hadn't looked carefully, if I hadn't really paid attention, I would have missed it. But there it was—a neatly cut square window right in the middle of the evergreen hedge. And a curtain hung over it. I swear it. A green velvet curtain hung in the window cut into the evergreen hedge. And the strange thing was that it looked like it had always been there.

We went closer. We squatted down. Later, Muulke would insist she saw it right away, but I know better than that. It took us both at least three seconds before we really saw anything. And when we realized exactly what we were seeing, we still couldn't believe our eyes.

The curtain looked like it was being pulled aside, and through the opening, a face stared out at us.

The Secret of the Hedge

AT THE END OF Sjlammbams Sahara stood a house. The house of Nine Open Arms.

We had no idea yet about Nienevee from Outside the Walls and Charley Bottletop, but from the moment we saw the face in the hedge, that would begin to change. Everything was about to change. We just didn't know that yet.

An arm slid out from the hedge. A green, grubby arm that reached right for me. I wanted to run, but I was rooted to the ground. I thought, *Now the hedge is going to grab me, now it's going to slurp me up, and nobody will ever hear of me again.*

But I hadn't reckoned with Muulke. Uttering a savage cry, she hurled herself forward at the arm and dug her teeth into it. Smothered moans came from behind the window. The arm tried to pull back, but it wasn't for nothing that Muulke had spent years playing the soldier in Threatened Treasure. She held on grimly as she was yanked forwards and pushed backwards, disappearing headfirst into the hedge and then coming out again. Twigs got stuck in her hair and her dress got caught on the branches, baring her legs well above her knees, but she hung on.

I wanted to shout something, do something, but my voice had vanished, and I stood there like a sack of coal.

"Muulke!" A voice cried.

Muulke was still half-hanging from the hedge, her feet at an angle, one elbow stuck among the branches. She was still hanging on to the arm, her mouth wide open.

"Muu-huulke!"

"What?" called Muulke.

"Muu-huulke?" the hedge said again.

"What?" I shouted back.

"*Miljaar!*" shouted Muulke.

His face was much thinner and even more wrinkled than the last time we had seen him. It was white as a candle and smeared with brown-green streaks. His hair was cut so short we could see the scalp. And then there was the beard—that wild, reddish-gray, tufty beard that hid his chin, the chin he used to call "as smooth as a pebble from the river, just have a feel." But the voice hadn't changed at all.

"Oompah Hatsi?" Muulke exclaimed.

Oompah Hatsi, the old button-chewer, was staring out through the window, and we were staring in.

"What are you doing? What's the matter?" Jess called from behind the hedge, panicked.

If she saw Oompah Hatsi in this state, she would have nightmares for the rest of her life.

"Nothing. Just wait by the gate," I called back, surprised at how calm my voice sounded. "We'll be right there."

"When?"

"Right away."

"Five minutes?"

"Okay."

Oompah beckoned. His arm, the arm Muulke had bitten, was bleeding.

"What does he want?" I asked.

"He wants us to come in, *iepekriet*," she said, as if Oompah wasn't a madman from the asylum, but a prim and proper aunt you could visit on a Sunday. As if he wasn't sitting inside a hedge (a hedge!), but in a house.

"Sorry, Oompah," I said as politely as I could. "But we have an awful lot of things to do. Another time perhaps." I turned to Muulke and whispered, "He might be really dangerous."

"*Sjiethoes!*" said Muulke. "This is Oompah Hatsi, the button king. Can't you see?"

"The button-chewer! Have you forgotten he was in the asylum?"

"But not any more."

"We're going," I said.

"In a minute."

"Now."

"In a minute."

"Oma Mei will be back at any moment," I said. "I think I can hear her."

Oompah looked from me to Muulke. He wiped his face with his arm, leaving a smear of blood behind on his cheek.

"We're going now," I grumbled. "Now!"

"Who were you talking to?" asked Jess when we got to the other side of the hedge.

"Nobody."

"That dead person?"

"Jess," I said. "There is no dead person."

"I saw a dead person." Jess's lip started to tremble again.

I looked at Muulke, who was angrily shaking her head.

"That wasn't a dead person," I said. "It was only Oompah Hatsi."

In hindsight, I now see it would have been better if I'd said we were talking to a thousand dead people. That they'd thrown us into a cauldron and boiled us alive. Jess turned so pale that I wouldn't have been at all surprised if she had fainted.

"You're not to tell anybody. It's our secret," said Muulke

"*Kwatsj*!" I said.

"He's going to gobble us up," Jess sobbed.

Muulke angrily clicked her tongue. "Oompah Hatsi? Ha!"

"He's crazy."

"No crazier than you."

"Oh no?"

"No!"

"Blabbermouth!"

"*Sjiethoes*!"

"Prune-face!"

"Scaredy-cat!"

"And now I'm absolutely going to tell," screamed Jess.

"They may be searching for him," I said. "We can't keep this a secret."

Muulke looked at me furiously. "Goody-goody!"

I shrugged.

But then Muulke the Soldier changed into Muulke the General. A cunning look came over her face. She crossed her arms.

"Do you want me to tell Oma Mei that you let Jess pull the cart with the water tubs?" Then, turning to Jess, "And do you want me to tell Oma Mei that you secretly loosen your straps?"

"What?" I gasped.

"That's mean!" Jess shouted. Her face turned beet red.

I grabbed Jess and could immediately feel that there was movement in the stays. "Are you crazy?"

"You say yourself that Oma Mei exaggerates."

"Exaggerates, yes. But she doesn't lie. Do you want to be as crooked as a capital C?"

"I am already," Jess snapped.

"Nonsense!" I snapped back.

"Jess will tighten them up," Muulke said soothingly. "And you won't say anything. Oompah is our secret. That's best for everyone. Isn't it?"

"Why can't we say anything?"

Muulke shrugged. "If Oma Mei keeps secrets from us, we can keep secrets from her. Fair's fair."

"Secrets? What secrets?" Jess wanted to know.

"Nothing," Muulke and I said together.

I gave in. Not just because I was scared stiff, but because it was a secret that couldn't remain one for very long. Oompah Hatsi would give himself away in no time at all. Nobody could live in a hedge barely a hundred feet away from our house without giving himself away. And certainly not anywhere near Oma Mei. Or so I thought.

When we got home, we found we had a visitor. Nol was sitting in the kitchen, nervously tapping on the table with a spoon. Muulke nudged me and pointed. He was wearing odd shoes.

"Not a problem," said Dad.

We looked at each other.

"What's not a problem?" asked Muulke.

Dad was pouring fresh hot water into the coffee pot. The water spilled but he didn't notice.

"Let me," I said.

Dad gave me a grateful look. He sat down next to Nol, patted him awkwardly on the back, and started drumming on the table with his fingers, in time with Nol. These two grown men suddenly looked younger than us.

"Oma Mei is going to stay overnight at Nol and Nettie's for a while," he said.

"Why?" Jess asked.

"Um…" Dad blushed.

"Why?" Jess repeated.

"You're too young for that," said Muulke.

"I know perfectly well that the stork doesn't exist," Jess said fiercely. "All I want to know is why."

"Because sometimes the new baby doesn't want to come," I said. I had heard Oma Mei say this to Fie's parents. I also knew that Nol's Nettie didn't have her babies easily. Two had already died at birth. That was why Nol was sitting there now wearing odd shoes and tapping away as if he was sending a telegram to God.

"This new baby isn't going to die," Muulke said soothingly. Nol turned paler than he already was.

And so it wasn't Oma Mei but Dad who made the rounds that evening. He tucked us in very carefully.

"Tighter."

He tightened the blankets a little.

"Tighter than that," said Muulke. "Oma Mei always pulls them so tight we can hardly breathe. And Jess has to lie on her back. You have to tell her she has to lie on her back."

"No, you have to tell Muulke not to snitch," said Jess.

Dad duly repeated everything. Then we each got a prickly, absent-minded kiss, and we heard him shuffle down the passage. It was strange. Dad was so much nicer than our grandmother, and yet we already missed her.

We twisted and turned and blamed each other for the blankets riding up and leaving our feet bare.

"Why do you undo the straps?" I asked when we finally were comfortable.

Jess shrugged.

"Well?" I asked.

"The thing doesn't squeak-creak so much that way."

"But your wreckbone could slip, you know that."

"Nothing has happened."

"Nothing?"

"Nothing."

But when she shifted, I could hear her groaning softly.

"Does it hurt?"

"No."

"Don't lie."

"I'm not lying."

"You groaned."

"You groan all the time yourself." She turned her head away.

In the middle of the night we were woken by her moans. Ten minutes later, in the pitch dark, Dad was running to the doctor's.

Waiting for Pigs to Fly

I SAID I WAS staying right there, that I wouldn't even think about it, but when Muulke, without so much as glancing back, squatted down and disappeared into the hedge, my feet suddenly developed a will of their own. Complaining loudly, I crawled in after her.

Oompah Hatsi the button-chewer's hedge-home had a secret entrance. If you didn't know about it, you'd never have been able to find it. It was hidden in the untidy gap in the hedge through which we went to the cemetery. To find it, we had to take two steps so we were standing exactly halfway between Sjlammbams Sahara and the cemetery. There the hedge looked as solid as a concrete wall, but if we squatted down and felt in the middle with our right hand, the branches gave way. Muulke was the one who had discovered this.

She crawled into the hedge on her hands and knees and was just about halfway in when she stopped. "Ouch, my hair! Fing, my hair!"

Cautiously, I poked my hands into the hole. It felt dry

and prickly. After a lot of effort, I managed to get Muulke's hair untangled.

"Keep your hands around your head," I said. "And come back out carefully."

"No way," said Muulke, and she disappeared inside.

Keeping my head as low as I could, I crawled in after her. Behind the branches that hid the entrance, there was a low, narrow passage that was carpeted with dry twigs, above which was a ceiling of more dry, brown twigs, through which small dots of light penetrated. To the side and above, where the green was less dense, the branches had been tied together with string to form an arch that made the tunnel feel more solid.

Something sharp pricked my bare knee, and I felt something tickling my neck.

"I hate you, Muulke Boon."

"Of course you do," said Muulke. "But without me you'd have such a boring life that one day you'd drop dead. Dying of boredom really happens. I heard the doctor say so."

I didn't want to think of Jess. Didn't want to remember how I'd felt when the doctor had come downstairs that morning. Even though he'd said it wasn't too bad this time. "A couple of weeks at the most," he'd said.

"It's my fault," I said to Muulke.

"Of course it isn't," Muulke replied. "She undid the straightener herself, didn't she? You weren't to know. And anyway, I did, so it's just as much my fault."

But no matter what Muulke said, I knew I should have looked after Jess more carefully.

At the end of the tunnel hung a green velvet curtain. When we pushed that aside, we both stopped for a minute. Before us lay a cave, a surprisingly large cave. You could almost stand up straight, and you could only touch both walls at once if you stretched your arms really wide. Here, too, the branches above me had been tied together with string. Now that I looked around, I suddenly understood why the hedge was so wide. Muulke realized it at the very same time.

"It isn't just one hedge at all," she said in surprise. "There are two of them."

So we discovered that there wasn't just a single row of pines but two rows, planted close together. Over the years they had grown together, but because the hedge was always pruned to look like a straight wall, we had never noticed it before. The hollow space had been made by cutting off the inside branches and leaving the outside ones.

"Did you make this, Oompah?" Muulke asked.

Oompah was sitting on the dusty ground. He was wearing a brass-band uniform jacket with dented buttons and sleeves that were too short. A battered straw hat was perched on his head. He looked at us and grumbled.

"All of this?" Muulke asked again.

She looked at the branches above our heads and tested their binds. Then she patted an old blanket lying in a corner and sat down on it.

"Come join me," she said.

But I wouldn't dream of it. God only knew how many lice and fleas were hiding there. I stood with my head bent forward and all I kept thinking was, *I'm inside the hedge. I'm inside the hedge. I'm actually inside the hedge.*

"Were you really in the madhouse, Oompah?" Muulke asked.

"You shouldn't ask things like that," I said.

"Why not?"

Oompah stared from Muulke to me and back again.

"Were you really there?" Muulke asked again.

He was silent.

"He doesn't want to talk about it, can't you understand that?"

The light coming through was dim and everything looked green: our clothes, our hair, the few specks of sunlight. The little cut-out window with the curtain was like one of the picture frames Oompah had hung up in our street such a long time ago. Only the view now was not of a crack in the wall but of a grassy field and a part of the grave without a name.

"He still has to get used to this," said Muulke. "Don't you, Oompah?"

The old button-chewer took a small pair of scissors from his jacket pocket and started snipping leaves and twigs above his head. The sleeve of his jacket creaked impressively when he stretched his arm.

"How did he get hold of those clothes?" I asked softly. I didn't know anything about madhouses, but I didn't think that everyone in there walked about in brass-band uniform jackets and straw hats.

"Stolen, of course," said Muulke. "Like those."

She pointed at the upturned wooden crate next to Oompah. On top, in a little tin dish, lay the better-luck-next-time cigars. Or what was left of them: three miserable little stumps. One had burst, and the other two were not much more than ash.

We didn't often have to run to school any more. We knew Sjlammbams Sahara like the back of our hand by now. For a head wind, I allowed an extra five minutes. For sand storms or mud pools, a quarter of an hour. The only thing that had made us leave half an hour early that winter was a heavy snowstorm. With summer coming, Muulke was the only catastrophe I had to take into account. She forgot the bread for the baker, lost her shoes or her hair ribbon. Now, the first day Jess was allowed back to school, Muulke hadn't combed her hair and it stuck up wildly in all directions.

"What on earth have you done to it?" I asked.

"How should I know?" said Muulke.

I took the hairbrush with me, and while we were walking I tried to straighten out her hair. Sister Theodora, who had Muulke's class, detested girls who were sloppy about their appearance. There were even rumors that she had cut off a girl's uncombed hair with the hedge clippers.

"Ouch! Not so hard," Muulke complained.

But I had no time for sympathy. "Too bad. And Jess, keep walking!"

Jess sighed.

The hedge was as straight and as solid as ever. Nothing betrayed its secret—the hollow at its center and the vagabond who lived there.

"Breathe," I said when we'd reached the spot where we always caught our breath.

"I'm really squeak-creaking," said Jess.

"Breathe."

She breathed.

"Is that all?" I said, relieved when I heard the awful noise. "Is that all you were carrying on about?"

"Get lost!"

After school, Oma Mei was waiting for us. She stood by the school gate with Nettie's bicycle. A wooden box with the shopping sat on the luggage carrier. She looked as if it was the most normal thing in the world for her to be standing there that way, but we knew how special it must be for her. She had always wanted a bicycle.

And even though her tongue was as fierce as ever ("Look out, Muulke! Don't lean against the bike. Jess, stand up straight. Do you want to grow as crooked as…"), I knew she was delighted to see us and that she missed us just as much as we missed her.

"How is Aunt Nettie?" we asked.

Oma Mei nodded, and that would have to do. She was wearing her hat with the rose. A tuft of white-gray hair had escaped from under it and was blowing a bit in the wind. For one long moment, I wanted to spread my arms wide and throw them around her and breathe in her scent.

"Is it going to take much longer?" Muulke asked.

"As long as God wills," Oma Mei replied curtly. She lifted the box from the luggage carrier and handed it to Muulke and me. "Straight home, do you hear? And stay together. Jess, stand up straight. Fing, make sure she doesn't slouch when she's walking. And don't forget to tell your father that Knoops has wire netting for the fly screens. Are you listening, Fing?" Meanwhile, she got the bike moving and slid onto the seat. She straightened her back, and the bike slowly wobbled away over the cobblestones. The hat with the rose teetered on her head.

We heard laughter behind us.

It was Fat Tonnie and her group.

"Well, look at that," they said. "There's scarecrow Jess with her scarecrow back."

"Ignore them," said Muulke. "Just ignore them."

We walked past the market, down Put Street, and through the Putse Gate.

"Why doesn't Fie ever wait for us any more?" I asked. "We never see her these days."

"No idea," said Jess.

"But you were talking with her yesterday, weren't you?"

"Yes."

"Didn't she say anything?"

"No."

"Change hands," said Muulke.

We changed hands and walked on.

"Shall we play Threatened Treasure this afternoon?" I asked.

Jess shrugged.

"You can be the Threat," I said. For a moment she looked brighter, but then her eyes went dull again.

"It's okay."

We had only just come home when Muulke wanted to go out again.

"Just to have a quick look," she whispered.

"We have to do the dishes first."

"We can do them later."

"It's on our list."

"It doesn't say when." Eyeing the basin, she called to Dad in the workshop that there was nowhere near enough water for that heap of dishes and could we please…

We could.

I grumbled, I complained, but I followed her anyway,

because the mere thought of her being alone with the button-chewer...

At first we thought Oompah was just keeping quiet. Muulke pushed the curtain aside and poked her head through the window. For a moment it looked as if she no longer had a head.

"*Miljaar*!"

"What?"

"He's gone."

I did my best to hide my relief. "He'll be back tomorrow," I said.

As there was nothing else to be done, Muulke inspected the grave without a name. She felt the stone, looked at it closely, even sniffed it.

"There's nothing on it."

"Told you so. Muulke?"

"No letters, no numbers, nothing."

"Muulke."

"Yes?"

"Why don't we ever visit Mom?"

Was it because of that lonely, nameless stone, which meant it could be anyone lying there? I don't know, but suddenly I felt the loss cut deep inside me, sharp as a knife.

"Because heaven is everywhere," Muulke said automatically. That was another typical opposite-of-worrying reply of Dad's: "Oh, *leeveke*, what would you want in a graveyard? Go and play and enjoy yourself. You can be sad for the rest of your life. And anyway, there's no need."

"Why not?" we'd ask.

"Because your mother is in heaven and heaven is everywhere."

Once a month Oma Mei put on her best clothes, put an apron, a sponge, and a short rake in a carry bag and caught the bus at the station. Our mother was buried in a cemetery in Dad's town, where she had lived with him and us until her death. I vaguely remembered visiting the cemetery once, but it was a long time ago. And whenever we asked Oma Mei if we could go, she said that a cemetery meant standing around and waiting and that children weren't good at that at all.

"But then why are we allowed to visit Opa Pei?" I asked.

Muulke shrugged. "Stop asking when you know the answer."

"I would really like to visit her sometime."

"You'll be waiting for pigs to fly," said Muulke indifferently.

"Do you remember our mother?"

"Everything."

"Like what?"

"Come on, there's nothing here for us."

"Like what?"

"Oh stop nagging. You're becoming just like Jess."

"You don't remember anything."

"She sang songs."

"All mothers do that."

"She ate with a knife and fork."

"What's that supposed to mean?"

Muulke stalked off angrily.

"You don't remember a thing," I called after her. "Not a single thing. Admit it, Muulke Boon. You don't remember a thing."

Something to Loosen His Tongue

FOR THE FIRST TIME in months, the angels seemed to be on my side, because the next day Oompah Hatsi was still missing.

And the following day.

And the day after that.

Muulke's mood went down and down. She became grumpy and grumbly like Oma Mei on her worst days, and she quarreled constantly with Jess.

"*Sjiethoes!*"

"Sourpuss!"

"Blabbermouth!"

"*Iepekriet!*"

"I've had just about enough of this!" shouted Oma Mei when she dropped in one Sunday after Mass. "If anyone shouts insults again, I'll personally wash out her mouth with soap."

I'm sure lots of grandmothers threaten their grandchildren in the same way, but ours was the only one I knew who actually did what she said.

Muulke and Jess grumbled a bit more, but they knew better than to do it aloud.

My hopes lasted exactly three days.

"He's back," Muulke whispered on the fourth day, as she poured out the dishwater.

My heart sank. "Are you sure? Perhaps you just thought—"

"You wish," Muulke cut in meanly. "Come on."

Oompah looked at us suspiciously from behind his little window. He was chewing on a lump of bread, and even from a distance, I could see it was moldy. It made me feel sick.

"Can we come in?" said Muulke.

Oompah waved his scissors threateningly. Snip! Snip!

When we came closer he started hissing. Breadcrumbs sprayed from his mouth and got stuck in his beard. I jumped back.

"I think we'd better go and get some water," I said.

This time I had no trouble getting Muulke to come along.

"He must go off foraging," she whispered with shining eyes. "That's why he's away all the time. He steals things, because, of course, he doesn't have any money. They took that away from him in the madhouse. They always do that. And then they hide the money in hollow trees. The gardens of madhouses are full of hollow trees."

I didn't bother asking where she'd gotten all of that. It would just have egged her on. So I didn't say anything, but shifted the tubs around till they felt secure. Then I pumped them full of water.

"You know what we should do?" Muulke said when I had finished.

"I guess you'll tell me anyway."

We gripped the handle and started pushing. I could feel Oompah's suspicious eyes on my back and had to stop myself from walking faster.

"We must help him," she said.

The opening in the hedge had started to grow over again, and we had to push hard to get the baby carriage through. Muulke kicked the thing and a splash of water hit my shoe.

"Watch what you're doing!" I shouted.

"Don't make such a fuss. Think about how we can help Oompah Hatsi." She made a virtuous face.

Nine Open Arms came into view, and in the late evening sunlight the weathered, crooked bricks seemed to glow from within. Swallows tumbled through the red and purple evening sky.

"You just want to keep him here," I said, "because you're worried he'll disappear and you won't have a tragical tragedy any more."

"You can think what you like."

"And you know as well as I do that we can help him best by telling. So he'll get into a decent home instead of sitting here in the hedge."

"No."

"Muulke, just listen…"

"Did you ever find that letter from the Rotterdam Banking Society?"

"Don't be stupid."

"Shall we ask Jess again if she wants to fetch water?"

"If you think you can threaten me, Muulke Boon, you're mistaken."

Muulke made a low stool by cutting three-quarters off the legs of an old chair from the small shed.

"So he won't have to sit on the floor, that poor man…"

"Yeah, right," I said. "If you're so concerned you've no doubt thought about the fact that the poor man will need to eat something, apart from moldy bread."

"The preserve jars," Muulke said instantly.

"Are you out of your mind? Oma Mei will notice right away."

"No, she won't," said Muulke. "She never goes into the cellar herself. The preserves are for winter. And if she does find out, we'll simply say we dropped one and it broke."

Already, I was scared stiff.

"Just one," I said. "Remember, just one. No more."

"Of course," said Muulke. "I'm not crazy."

She snatched two jars off the shelf.

"What are you doing?" Jess asked.

"Nothing for *sjiethoezer*," said Muulke.

"What do you want with those preserve jars?"

"Not telling."

"Then I'm going to tell Oma Mei."

"Are your straps tightened properly?" Muulke asked sweetly.

Jess moved around in her straightener. The leather and the buckles squeaked and creaked. Jess probably meant it to sound triumphant, but it didn't.

"They're for Oompah Hatsi," I said. "So he has something to eat."

"Are you going there now?"

I nodded.

"I'm coming."

"Coming?" I said in surprise.

"It's up to you," said Muulke. "As long as you don't carry on like a *sjiethoes*."

"Look what we've got," said Muulke. "Look what we've brought for you! Nice? What would you like? Pears? Asparagus?"

She was talking in a tone I'd never heard from her. Very softly, quietly. Snip. Oompah's scissors went again. Snip. But the sound was softer, less threatening.

"I've got something else," said Muulke. She was sitting on the short grass, her arms around her knees. "Jess, could you get it, please."

Jess, who had stayed at a safe distance, brought out the little stool. She gave it to me, and I passed it to Muulke.

"Nice, isn't it?" said Muulke. "So you can sit comfortably. Wouldn't you like to sit nice and comfortably?" She got up halfway and let herself down onto the stool. "Ah, lovely. I'm so glad to sit down!"

She sounded like Oma Mei; her voice had even gone a little croaky.

Oompah watched her every move carefully. The scissors no longer snip-snipped. Suddenly he beckoned.

"He's remembered who we are," said Muulke. "Come on."

Jess stayed by the carriage.

More branches had been sewn together with careful cross-stitches. The floor of the hollow was now covered with a layer of straw and a small rug. In a corner, there was a large burlap sack. Muulke immediately started crawling towards it.

"Don't," I said.

She opened it right away. "Look!"

In the sack were a small box, a bundle of rags, a damaged lampshade, a cup, knives and spoons, and a fox-fur collar, similar to the ones fashionable ladies often wore. What could be done with this fox was a question, since it was a moth-eaten beast with beads where its eyes used to be. It even looked like it was grinning through crumbling teeth.

"Stole it all, I bet," Muulke whispered in my ear.

While the button-chewer was removing the lid of a conserve jar with greedy hands, I kept an eye on Jess through the little window.

Oompah slurped up the contents: pears in syrup. The juice dripped through his filthy beard, and he made loud smacking sounds. I could hardly hide my disgust, but Muulke looked as if she'd captured some exotic animal.

"Nice, Oompah? Did you like that?"

Oompah picked up his scissors and snipped once.

"Do tell me you liked it," Muulke cajoled.

Oompah snipped twice with his scissors.

She frowned. "Why won't he say something?"

"How should I know."

"He said something before."

"When before?"

"When we were fighting. He said my name then."

"Oompah, say my name again."

Oompah grinned.

"Perhaps he only says something when he absolutely has to say something," I said.

Oompah snipped again.

"He's saying something now," said Jess. She'd come a bit closer.

"What did you say?" asked Muulke.

"That he's saying something now," said Jess, all the while keeping a nervous eye on the button-chewer.

"If he is, he's doing it awfully quietly," said Muulke.

"He talks with his scissors," said Jess.

Muulke looked at her stupidly.

"One snip for yes," said Jess. "And two snips for no."

Muulke was about to tap her forehead with her finger, but she stopped. She stared thoughtfully at Jess, then at Oompah.

"Is that right, Oompah?"

The button-chewer stared at the ceiling. The hand holding the scissors went up slowly.

Snip.

"Or is it all *kwatsj*?"

Snip. Snip.

"You're a genius!" Muulke exclaimed, staring at Jess.

That Saturday night, Theodoor Guillaume Anna Theresa Rutten was born, and according to Oma Mei he was a story that almost didn't begin. Holding him by his feet, our grandmother had plunged him by turns into deep tubs of cold and hot water, but he had just stared at her stubbornly while his face had turned a deeper and deeper blue. Just when everybody had thought he was about to be off to heaven, he started yelling and kept on yelling for the next three days.

We went to see him in our Sunday dresses. Aunt Nettie was in bed. She had her hair undone, which made us a bit shy, because we had only ever seen her with her hair in a bun. We ate plum tart and looked jealously at the tightly swaddled little baby.

All day long, visitors came and went. Our grandmother said we should go home, but we didn't feel like going home. Years seemed to have passed by the time she finally packed up her knitting and her bag of clothes and said goodbye. Outside, she gave the seat of the bike a regretful little tap. Then, at long last, she walked with us out of the town.

We fluttered about her like butterflies. We squabbled about who would carry her bag and kept a careful eye on her. As if she wasn't our solid, stocky grandmother (with feet so wide she could only wear men's shoes), but a feather or a leaf in the wind.

When I saw the untidy black-and-red roof of Nine Open Arms appear in the distance, I sighed with relief.

Now that Theodoor Rutten had safely arrived into this world, Oma Mei turned her good eye back on us. Along with her swivel-eye, which forecast trouble.

"Where are you off to?"

"To fetch water."

"All three of you?"

"It's easier that way."

Oma Mei looked at the tubs.

"Do you think we're fish?"

"But..."

"We've still got plenty of water. If you're bored, I've got plenty else for you to do."

I didn't really mind. I didn't care how often Muulke said

that it was Oompah, our old neighbor, because he was still a madman, no matter what. Secretly, I kept hoping that Oma Mei would find out about him. And that would almost certainly have happened if Oompah hadn't learned to practically turn himself into a stone.

"Because he has escaped, of course," said Muulke. "The madhouse keepers are looking for him. That's why he keeps quiet."

"Where on earth did you get that idea from?" I asked.

"He said so himself," said Muulke.

I didn't take her words very seriously. Oompah may have been able to talk with his scissors, but that didn't mean he actually said very much. And whenever Muulke became too curious, he just stared up at the roof of his hedge-home and muttered something.

"He has to learn how to talk all over again," said Muulke.

"He can stay silent as far as I'm concerned."

"Do you want him to stay mad forever? If we can teach him to talk again, he'll automatically become normal again. That poor man..."

"Saint Muulke!" I pronounced.

She took no notice. "We'll have to give him something."

"What are you talking about?"

"Something to loosen his tongue."

"What?"

"Brandy or something. Alcohol, *iepekriet.*"

There were times when I knew exactly how Oma Mei felt.

"I believe you're going seriously around the bend, Muulke Boon," I said. "Have you forgotten that the last time he drank he ended up in the madhouse?"

"But he was talking then," said Muulke.

"If you dare, I'll tell Oma Mei everything. And I won't care what you tell her."

"Do you even believe that yourself?" Muulke glared at me, but I didn't lower my eyes. This time I wasn't going to give in. Enough was enough.

Suddenly she fluttered her eyelids, pouted her doll's mouth, and smiled. "Only joking!" She threw her arms around me. "Where in heaven's name would we get brandy anyway? Oma Mei won't even allow a glass of beer into the house."

It was midnight. Next to me, Jess moved her leg restlessly over the bare wood of her bed. The lamb's wool blanket had half-slipped off, so I straightened it. In her sleep, she looked even more like a little bird than usual. She lay on her side with her shoulders pulled up high and her chin against her chest. Her small, sharp nose was like a beak. I carefully put my hand on her shoulder and walked two fingers over her nightgown, down to her wreckbone. I found it right away. One vertebra, just a little smaller than the rest, that stuck out just a little. Feeling Jess's wreckbone was like coming home. Especially in the dark. Especially in the middle of the night.

Discovered!

THEN THINGS BEGAN to go wrong again, and we came very close to causing a tragical tragedy ourselves.

On the first warm evening, we ate under the linden tree. Oma Mei had ordered the table to be put outside. She had made four fruit pies that morning, which she'd sent to the bakery to be baked. She did that quite often to make some extra money. This time the order was for a wedding, but the bridegroom had run off.

"This cigar is a fast burner," said Sjeer. "Two puffs and your nose is on fire."

Piet and Krit were sitting opposite him, pulling apart their own cigars. The table was covered with tobacco leaves, fillers, knives, and molds, but Oma Mei hadn't objected once.

"It looks like there's been an explosion," said Muulke.

"All will be well," said Dad, but his own cigar was like a badly stuffed sausage, plump in the middle and empty at the ends.

Jess, Muulke, and I were sitting on the grass. We'd eaten so much fruit pie that we felt exhausted. Muulke lay on her back with her knees to the left and her head to the right. She looked like she'd fallen to pieces.

"Shall we play Threatened Treasure?" Jess suggested.

"Childish," said Muulke.

"Last week you didn't think it was childish."

Muulke stuck out her tongue. "I'm eleven."

"Nowhere near yet," I said.

"Nearly."

"You're not."

"Am so."

"Muulke, stop squabbling," said Oma Mei without looking up from her knitting. It was too warm for the time of year. The sky was cloudy, and the air felt as hot and as thick as pea soup.

For the first time in a long while, the Crocodile was opened again that evening. It was a story about our mother with the rag-doll heart from when she was a child. It took place on the feast day of Saint Rosa, the patron saint of the town.

Oma Mei had been ill. Fortunately, she had set up the little house altar outside their porch the day before so that the bishop would be able to bless it during the procession. But then the coalman's horse had bolted, cart and all. (There were whispers that Saint Rosa was angry because the coalman had been working as if it was any old day.) The cart had tipped over, spilling all the coal and *sjlamm* and blocking the road past their house. None of the clergy wanted to get their vestments dirty, so they took a different route.

When our mother got wind of that, she didn't waste time worrying. Instead, she stuffed the candles, the candlesticks, the plaster statue of the Virgin, the rosary, and the tablecloth into her basket and hoisted the heavy little oak table onto her back. She'd climbed over the coal and *sjlamm*, pushed her way through the crowd, and found a spot.

"And so we got the blessing after all," said Oma Mei. "And because your mother was on her knees behind the altar, nobody could see that her white dress and shoes were pitch-black."

We stared at the tiny, curled-up photo. It showed a lot of girls, all dressed in white. They wore coronets of white roses on their heads. One of them was our mother. She stood at the back. Our grandmother pointed her out, but the face was so small it could have been anyone.

"Is Mr. Wetsels burning stuff?" Oma Mei asked suddenly. We sniffed the air. Something was definitely burning. And now that we were quiet, we couldn't just smell it, we could also hear a soft crackling, and then, suddenly, a loud, sharp crack, and the clinking of glass.

"It's coming from the cemetery," said Eet, who was already running in the direction of the sound.

In a fright, I looked at Jess and Muulke.

By the gate, Eet turned toward us. "The hedge!" he shouted.

Oma Mei was the most level-headed. She shouted for the carriage and loaded it up with tubs and buckets. Muulke was sent to fetch blankets. Then we raced to the opening in the hedge.

If the wind had been in the wrong direction, we never would have been able to get to the pump. But the wind blew the fire away from the gap, so the way through was still open, though full of smoke. Pushing and pulling the carriage through the hedge, we ran to the pump as fast as we could.

The crackling became a roar. Already, the flames were rising high, which was strange because it was living wood. Piet said later that it probably was because of all the straw at the bottom of the hedge.

Dad was pumping and our brothers were filling the vases they'd grabbed from the gravestones. "Here!" they shouted to us. "Here!"

Muulke, Oma Mei, Jess, and I kept farthest away from the fire, but even from there, it was a terrifying sight. The fire was an all-devouring, all-destroying light. We couldn't look through it. The glare of the flames was reflected in the sweat-covered faces of our brothers. After what seemed like an eternity of pumping and putting out the fire, just when I thought I'd had it, when my hands and arms had gone numb, when I thought the fire was going to win, it finally started to lose ground, until all that was left was a long, smoldering stretch of charred hedge.

Our brothers and Dad slapped each other on the back. Eet and Piet were already eagerly rehashing the whole fire. What if the wind had been like this or that, or what if we'd had only two buckets and one vase...

We heard the sound of someone sobbing.

"Jess, please," said Oma Mei, annoyed.

The sobbing became louder.

"It isn't as bad as all that," said Oma Mei.

"But I'm not doing anything," Jess objected.

We turned around.

There was Muulke, her sooty hands covering her face, crying as if she was trying to personally put out all the fires of hell with her tears. She stood near the hedge. The branches looked like charred skeletons, and through the openings created by the fire, we now could clearly see Oompah Hatsi's old home, or at least what remained of it: the chair with its cut-off legs and the rug, both scorched black; a couple of branches tied together, missed by the fire; a heap of soot-covered thick shards from the conserve jars. And more shards. Bright-blue shards.

We found Oompah sitting in the middle of Sjlammbams Sahara. His clothes were steaming, his short coppery-gray hair was singed, and the stump of a better-luck-next-time cigar was in his mouth. His eyebrows were also missing. Maybe that's why he had such a surprised look on his face. He was holding the fox fur in his hands. It was completely scorched, the eyes had melted, and only its teeth were recognizable.

"*Miljaar!*" Piet, Eet, Sjeer, and Krit said together.

We all were staring at Oompah Hatsi, the smoldering button-chewer, who stared back like an overgrown baby. He was blind drunk on the cherries in brandy from Fie's parents' blue preserving jar. The jar Muulke had stolen, hoping for a bit of tragical tragedy.

A Long Road

"IT'S NO STORY FOR children, " said Oma Mei. "That's for sure."

We were sitting around the kitchen table. Our hair and our clothes still reeked of smoke. We were covered in soot and ash. The kerosene lamp drew a tight circle of light around us, dividing each of us into two halves, one dark and one light.

In the silence, we could hear the deep snoring that came through the crack in the living room door.

Staggering, supported by Dad on one side and by Sjeer and Piet on the other, the button-chewer had come into Nine Open Arms.

"Has he burned his legs?" Muulke had asked. "Is that what's wrong?" She had fluttered around him until Oma Mei had pushed her away.

"He's just blind drunk," she had said curtly.

That wasn't entirely true, because when she went in to take care of him, it had involved bandages, scissors, and vaseline. But Oma Mei had resolutely shut the connecting door. As far as that was possible with a door that wouldn't quite shut.

"He must be terribly burnt," said Muulke, her eyes glittering. "Next thing you know, an arm or a leg will fall off, just like that. Boom!"

Jess, with her hands over her ears, was loudly shouting for Dad to make Muulke stop, but he was still blinking his eyes from the surprise.

"What's that button-chewer doing here?" he asked.

I could see the answer forming on Muulke's lips.

"Spare us your tragedies," I yelled.

"It's no story for children," Oma Mei said again while she put away the first-aid box.

"I'm nearly eleven," Muulke said right away.

"Chairs on four legs, please."

Muulke straightened her chair.

Oma Mei sent Jess upstairs, but strangely enough she said nothing to us. Her hands were still shiny with vaseline when she pushed her own chair back and sat down.

"Did you know Oompah was here?" Dad asked.

"I suspected it," said Oma Mei.

"Why didn't you say anything?"

"And let that poor man be picked up by the police?"

"He's stolen things."

"Reject cigars!" Oma Mei jeered.

We heard Oompah let out a plaintive sigh from the bedroom. For a while, she said nothing more. Nobody dared speak.

"Reject cigars," Oma Mei said again, but softly this time. "The poor devil. Who knows what could have happened."

"It would have been his own fault," said Dad, still a bit

angry. "He shouldn't have gotten pickled. I can't bear thinking what could have happened."

"Nothing has happened," said Oma Mei firmly. "You don't really know what's what. Nobody drinks without a reason."

It was strange to hear so much understanding coming from our grandmother's mouth.

"And why is he no longer in the madhouse?" Eet wanted to know.

"Maybe they let him out," said Oma Mei. "Or he ran away. I've got no idea."

"Why didn't you say anything?" Dad repeated.

There was a brief silence.

"It's no story for children," our grandmother said for the third time. "That's for sure." She looked at us.

"But they're awake now, " said Dad. "And if we send them upstairs, they'll listen secretly anyway."

We were surprised by Dad's words. We'd never known that he knew. But Oma Mei clearly hadn't guessed, as we could see from her face.

Again, for a while, she said nothing. But she looked from me to Muulke and back again, and I could see she had made up her mind.

"You have to grow up sometime."

I watched Muulke, who was sitting bolt upright, a perfect picture of good behavior. She hardly dared breathe, afraid Oma Mei would change her mind. A scorched twig was still stuck in her hair.

"Been there for a long time," said Oma Mei.

"Who?" asked Sjeer.

"Oompah, of course," said Muulke.

Oma Mei silently stared out through the kitchen window. We followed her gaze. The sandy road glowed in the early moonlight.

"I think she's talking about Sjlammbams Sahara," I said.

Oma Mei nodded.

"It was here already when your mother was little. It was here already when I was a child. It was here already long before I was born."

She tilted her head, as if she was listening to something far off.

"Ask me," she said.

PART TWO

Nienevee from Outside the Walls

Ask If She Was Welcome

FROM GERMANY, A SMALL group of travelers came along Sjlammbams Sahara. It was the end of August, 1863, and it had been raining nonstop for four days. In places, the road was like a small creek. Clumps of grass and ears of corn floated everywhere.

First came a cart, pulled by five dogs. This was followed by a horse-drawn caravan. Then came three more small, heavily loaded wooden carts. The travelers turned into a small field just outside the town.

It wasn't long before the townspeople found out.

The townspeople disliked travelers. It had always been that way.

"They need to know who's boss," they said. "They need to know people can't simply settle down anywhere just because they feel like it."

The biggest loudmouths gathered their courage at Nol's bar on the corner. They came with four table legs from the workshop of Lame Krit, the furniture maker, "Just in case." They arrived at the field with cold, wet feet. The travelers were having a meal. There were five of them: two men, one with a beard, one with a moustache, a woman with a boxer's nose, and a boy who sat on a box next to a girl. The man with the moustache wiped his mouth with the cloth on his knees. The woman brought out wine. Seven glasses were set and the wine was poured.

"We would like to share a drink with you," the man said to the townspeople. "But a few of our glasses were lost on our last trip. And guests come first."

The townspeople clenched their jaws. They said once more that people couldn't simply settle down anywhere just because they felt like it.

"Making a nuisance of themselves, right?" said the man.

The townspeople said that would really be the end. And that it would be best if everyone observed the proper customs.

"Know what we mean?" they added.

The man with the moustache nodded, and the townspeople went home satisfied.

Having refused a glass of wine had given them a great thirst, so they had a few at Nol's.

"They need to know their place," they said to anyone who cared to listen. "Then there won't be any trouble."

The following day they discovered that the travelers were still there. Again they picked up the table legs, and again they walked down Sjlammbams Sahara.

Since the arrival of the travelers, there had been no more rain, but the road was still slippery and soggy. It was Sunday. Morning Mass was over but afternoon Benediction was still to come, so the men were still in their Sunday suits. Before they'd gone any distance at all, their trouser cuffs and their shoes were filthy. Maybe that's why things came to a head.

After only three sentences were spoken, the first threats were uttered. Then the travelers brought out their dogs.

"Hellhounds," the loudest mouths shouted when they were back at Nol's. "With jaws like bear traps. What can you do against that? We have our children to think of. Nothing to do with cowardice."

After a half-dozen beers, Lame Krit, the loudest mouth of all, knew just how to make the intruders change their tune. One by one, he pressed grains of rat poison into a sausage that he gave to his son, Charley.

Charley had just turned twelve and was Lame Krit's only surviving child. Three older sons and Lame's wife had perished in the great town fire of 1861, which had been caused by a lightning strike. The furniture workshop had burned to the ground. The town council paid for a new workshop, and the townspeople contributed household goods, food, and even furniture, because nothing had survived. The fire had given Lame Krit his nickname; he had been crippled when he was hit by a falling rafter while trying to rescue his wife from the burning house. It had also turned him into a bitter man. Three strong, healthy sons had perished and the only one left was little Charley, an afterthought, with hands as slight as a dressmaker's.

The only thing was for Charley to grow up fast and become a man, and Lame Krit knew how to make that happen.

"Make sure not a single one of those travelers' dogs will ever bark again," he said.

The plan turned into a disaster.

Charley hadn't even reached the Putse Gate with its guards when he was overtaken by Dimdog. Dimdog was meant to be their watchdog, but she wasn't fierce enough. Lame wanted to drown her, but Charley had managed to prevent that so far. Dimdog was small, with a constantly slobbering mouth and dark, dumb eyes. Most of the time she was locked in the coal shed at the workshop, her short snout poking through the hole in the door. As soon as she had half a chance, though, she'd escape.

Dimdog was crazy about Charley. And she was even crazier about sausages.

Charley tried to make her go home, but he wasn't really sorry when she wouldn't. He didn't like Sjlammbams Sahara in the dark; he had heard too many stories that ended badly. And he knew that as long as he kept the poisoned sausage under his coat, Dimdog was in no danger.

"The gate will be locked at eleven, Charley Bottletop," said the guards. "After that, you can only look from outside as we sleep soundly inside."

It was a strange night, the night that Charley Bottletop and Dimdog set out to poison the travelers' dogs. There must have been wind up in the sky, because large clumps of clouds raced across it. But down on the ground, at the start of Sjlammbams Sahara, there was hardly a breath of air. It was so still you could hear the foxes yipping in the cornfield.

Charley clutched the sausage to his chest with one hand and held the chair leg with the other. They passed the cornfield, the field of beets, and finally came to the spot where earthen banks hid the road and led downward. On the left embankment stood a blackened oak tree; on the right, dense blackberry bushes.

Dimdog stopped.

"Come on," said Charley. But Dimdog stayed right where she was, even when Charley slid farther along the muddy path. He pulled out the sausage. Dimdog may not have seen it, but she could certainly smell it. Wagging her whole body, she came toward Charley.

At the last bend in the road, he stopped. From there, he could see the field where the travelers were camping. He saw a burning lantern, dangling from a stick attached to the caravan. White underpants hung on a laundry line. He couldn't see the dogs. Apart from the horse tied to a linden tree a little farther along, there was no sign of life.

"They'll be lying under the caravan," Lame Krit had told him. "Be careful not to walk downwind."

Charley wet his finger, but he couldn't feel the direction of the wind. He used his belt to tie Dimdog to a tree. She whimpered softly, protesting.

"Shush, Dimdog, shush!"

He went as close to the field as he dared. He still couldn't see the dogs, but sensed they were there. Even though he was small, he had to walk bent over to make sure he wouldn't be seen. Crawling wasn't possible; the ground was too soggy. It was hard work and slow going with the chair leg in one hand, the sausage in the other. Now that he no longer had a belt on, his pants sagged down on his hips.

"When I grow up, I'm going to be just as tall as Tei," Charley had said. It wasn't long after the fire, and he wanted to comfort his father. Tei had been his oldest brother.

Lame Krit had hit him, giving him a bloody nose. "Trees will learn to walk before then, Bottletop."

Charley hadn't objected when Lame gave him the sausage. Not only because it wasn't a good idea to refuse him anything, but because Charley himself wanted to grow up as fast as possible. The sooner he grew up, the sooner he could pack his bags and leave. That's why he had just nodded.

He felt the sweat prickling on his back while he forced himself to move closer. Step by step, he was improving his chances of aiming the sausage at the right spot. He went by way of the linden tree. The horse barely moved its ears it was so deeply asleep. When Charley reached the tree, he stopped. From there it was no more than a dozen paces to the caravan. He still couldn't see the dogs, only the pitch-black space between the caravan and the grass.

Then...There was something. He wasn't sure...He held his breath.

He thought he saw something glittering. *Dogs' eyes?*

The darkness shifted. Something moved! How many hellhounds were there, anyway? What if they had picked up his scent? What if they suddenly dashed out? He began to panic. He pressed himself against the tree, not daring to go any farther. The smallest movement would give him away. How could he get out the sausage, let alone throw it?

It was Lame Krit's words that made him move again: "Trees will learn to walk before then, Bottletop."

He took deep breaths, once, twice, once more, deeper this time, and then he did it. One step, two steps, knees bent so low his legs trembled. He took aim and threw. The sausage whizzed through the air, a beautiful throw. It bounced through the grass, rolled under the caravan, and disappeared from sight.

It happened so smoothly it looked like a conjuror's trick. He glowed with pride. Lame Krit would come down a peg or two now. He was in for a surprise, would even be at a loss for words: *My dear boy...*

Then the sky fell on top of him.

At least, that's what it felt like.

So suddenly did it happen, he didn't have time to brace himself. He toppled over, face down. His breath was knocked out of him. He wanted to heave himself up, but a hand was pressing down on his head. He wanted to scream, but all he could do was choke on grass and mud.

Ask Who Was Given
a Townies' Welcome

THERE LAY CHARLEY BOTTLETOP, failed dog killer, his face down in the mud. He couldn't catch his breath. Just as he was about to faint, the hands let go of him. Gasping for air, he rolled sideways. Someone twisted his arm behind his back. He opened his eyes. The mud stung, but he had to see.

A boy's grinning face hovered just above him. The boy was not alone; opposite Charley a girl crouched in the grass. It was hard to tell how old she was. She was wearing a coat that was too big, and she had a doll's face, but there was nothing doll-like about the eyes that glared back at him. They were so dark that the blackness under the caravan seemed pale by comparison.

"So you almost didn't throw it," said the girl. "You almost went back home." She spoke as if they had been having a conversation that had been briefly interrupted. She nestled into her coat, pulling it more tightly around her and tucking in her feet. "We were sitting in the linden tree. We fell on top of you. Accidently."

"Lexidently," the boy echoed, laughing softly. Charley felt his arm being twisted further with every chuckle.

"You have no right to be camping here," he said sharply.

The girl didn't reply. She was staring at a spot in the grass. It took Charley a while to realize she wanted him to look there, too. And then he saw it.

There lay the sausage. The sausage with the rat poison. None of it had been eaten.

"Our dogs won't accept anything from strangers. Not even when they're very hungry. My father trains them. He won't let me see how. He says it's not suitable for girls." She looked him in the face. He heard the boy sniffle.

"You should have given me the sausage," said the girl. "They would take it from me. I could have fed them." She moved her head closer. "Is that mud or blood? My brother is always falling out of trees, you know. He dragged me along. We fell on top of you."

The boy laughed again. His hands let go of Charley, but immediately the chair leg came down gently on his shoulder, so he didn't dare try to escape.

"Where's your dog?" asked the girl.

"What dog?"

But she had already stood up. The coat was wide in the shoulders and the sleeves hung way down. She whistled softly. That was all Dimdog needed; Dimdog was everybody's friend. She whimpered and rustled among the shrubs, as if to say: "Quick! Come, quick!"

"What a lonely-sounding whimper," said the girl. "Dogs can't take being alone. Cats can, but they eat birds. I don't like cats. Only when they're asleep. Are you all on your own, doggie? Is that why you're crying? I'm coming, doggie, I'm coming."

Charley wasn't taken in for a moment. But Dimdog... The noise from the shrubs sounded like at least three dogs.

The boy had a strange elongated head, as if it had been squashed by something. There were no teeth left in his upper jaw. He peered anxiously in the direction the girl had disappeared.

She reappeared with Dimdog.

The dog could tell that something wasn't quite right, but she pretended it was. She yawned in an exaggerated way, stretched her forelegs, and took a little leap in an everything-is-lovely sort of way. *Dimdog isn't so dumb after all*, Charley thought.

There was a sound from under the caravan. Charley saw two pale little dog snouts. Then a leg. He heard squealing, or was it growling? Were those the dogs? Those scrawny little things? Were they the "hellhounds" Lame Krit had been going on about? With "jaws like bear traps"?

The girl clicked her tongue. The dogs disappeared.

"They want to join in," she said. "But that would mean puppies."

The boy smirked.

"Quiet," said the girl, looking at the caravan.

Quiet? thought Charley. *Who for?*

"My father beat someone to death once," she said before he could even open his mouth to call for help.

"Lexidently," said the boy.

Maybe that talk about beating was a lie, but Charley had no intention of finding out.

"Accidently," said the girl, with a sinister smile. She stroked Dimdog, who meanwhile had lay down and was staring stupidly from Charley to the girl, from the girl to Charley, from Charley to the sausage.

"Guests first," she said.

Before Charley could do anything, she slackened the belt, his belt. For one tenth, no, one hundredth, of a second, he dared hope that Dimdog wouldn't be that stupid after all. But then it was all over. The dog hurled herself forward and gobbled up the sausage, the poisonous sausage, the sausage chock-full of rat poison. Drool dripped onto the grass. Chomp, chomp, one half, chomp, chomp the other half. She smacked her lips, peered greedily at the grass, and then looked at the girl and at Charley.

"Rat poison?"

He nodded, in a daze.

"Lexidently," said the boy. "Now dead?"

"No," she said. "First cramps and fits, then blood, then dead."

He was forever going to remain Bottletop, which was bad. But the poison in Dimdog was much worse.

"Townies' welcome," said the girl.

"What?"

She explained slowly, as if he was a slow student. "Townies' welcome" was what the travelers called harassment by townspeople. Nearly every town or village did it. There were many different kinds of townies' welcomes. Townspeople were inventive. They would, for instance, refuse a camping permit. Or threaten to put your children into an orphanage if you stayed any longer. Oh, and there was poison, of course. Not for the travelers, but very good for their horses. And dogs. There was nothing to be done against many kinds of townies' welcomes, but you could do something about poison. Sometimes.

She was silent.

"Is there anything you can do against this poison?"

he asked.

"If you're quick. Sometimes." She turned her eyes to the chair leg. "Make it yourself?"

Charley nodded.

She ran her fingers over the polished timber. "Can you make a whole chair?"

Was she pulling his leg?

"I do have money," he said. "At home."

She shook her head and tapped the chair leg.

He couldn't understand what was going on. But there was no need, really. She was saying she could help.

"Good," he said. "Give."

"Give?"

"The antidote for the poison."

"And never see you again?"

"I swear I'll come back."

"Dog-murderer's honor, I suppose?" Again she shook her head. "She's staying here with me."

"No," said Charley.

Dimdog whimpered.

"First cramps and fits," she said. "Then blood, then dead."

He broke into a cold sweat.

The girl stood up, picked up the belt, and walked off to the caravan with his dog.

Without looking back, she said, "Come back in a week. With the chair. Wait by the split oak tree. In the afternoon. If you don't come…"

As Charley walked home he cried so hard that the rabbits by the side of the road ran away. When he got to the Putse Gate, the guards had already locked up the town, and no matter how hard he banged, there was no way he could get back inside.

The next day, the news was all over the town. The travelers' dogs were sick! Farmer Kalle had seen them that morning, puking and shivering, standing in a small group among the corn, retching horribly.

"Sick as in deadly ill?" Lame Krit asked greedily. "As in dying?"

With a sour expression on his face, Farmer Kalle pointed at the tear in his trousers. "Don't count on it," he said. "There was plenty of life left in those vicious curs."

In the workshop, Charley said, "Perhaps the poison was too old."

Lame Krit cursed like a maniac. Out of sheer fury, he made Charley sand remnants, a terrible job, because the wood was full of nasty splinters that constantly got under his fingernails and broke off when he tried to pull them out. But that was as far as Lame Krit went.

Later, when Charley passed the coal shed, there was no short little snout pushing through the hole in the middle of the door, as if the door itself had a nose.

"Dimdog!" Charley cried.

That evening, he started work on the chair.

Meanwhile, Lame Krit got a lecture from the parish priest, who had "by chance heard stories" about "peculiar practices" used against the travelers in the field. "Just think about it, Lame," said the priest, who had no wish for a quarrel with God. After all, the travelers were all staunch believers.

Afterwards, the man of God had a long talk with the travelers, who then broke camp and let themselves be shown to a new site, far from the road, halfway into the forest, and even darker and soggier than the last.

The townspeople were content.

Ask Who Should
Know Her Place

A WEEK LATER, CHARLEY walked through the Putse Gate and down Sjlammbams Sahara carrying the chair.

She was waiting with Lexidently. In the daylight, she looked even stranger than at night. She had a pale, freckled face, and her hair was the color of polished copper.

The burnt oak tree stood out black against the blue sky.

"My dog?" asked Charley.

"My chair?" asked the girl.

Did she think he was a halfwit? "Hidden," he said. "How do I know she isn't dead?"

"How do I know you've actually made the chair?"

They glared at each other. Lexidently was getting restless. He climbed up the embankment, scratched at the charred bark of the oak, and swung from a branch that broke right off. He tumbled down the embankment like a bag of bones and came to rest at their feet.

"Come along," said the girl.

She started climbing up the embankment. Lexidently immediately jumped up and followed her.

At the top of the embankment was a field where an unfamiliar crop was growing. It was there by order of Van Wessum, the brick manufacturer. He had brought the seeds back with him from America, after he had tried in vain to build a new life for himself on the other side of the ocean.

The landscape sloped gently, down and up. Everywhere, stretching as far as the distant Kollenberg hill, stood tall golden corncobs covered with pale leaves.

They cleared themselves a path, led by the girl, who pulled the much taller Lexidently along behind her by his shirttail.

When the ground started to rise again, Charley suddenly stepped from amidst the corn into a small, flat clearing of brown, crumbly earth. In the center, tied to a thick wooden post, lay Dimdog. She was restrained by a rope and Charlie's belt was tied around her snout. Dimdog blinked, wagged her tail, lifted her head slowly, and lowered it again.

She was alive.

Alive!

"The chair," said the girl.

When he returned, the belt had gone from around Dimdog's snout. Lexidently stroked the dog and carefully wiped something from the corner of her eye with the tail of his shirt. But the girl didn't notice. She didn't notice anything. Charley had never seen anyone so pleased with a chair (made only from remnants!) who also tried so hard to hide it.

"Is that all?" she asked, but she was already holding out her hands.

She took the chair from him, felt its weight. She must have found it satisfactory, for her dark eyes lit up for a moment. Then she walked around the clearing, holding the chair carefully out in front of her, as if it was a child she wanted to put down in a safe spot. She tried it here and there. Eventually, she seemed satisfied and put it down.

For the rest of his life, Charley would carry that image with him.

Another image that would stay with him was of the chair sinking slowly into the ground the moment she sat down on it. Its thin rear legs sank into the soft earth. Then the chair slipped back, and she slipped with it. Before she could regain her balance, she was on her back. Charley burst out laughing, he couldn't help it. For a moment she looked at him furiously, but then Lexidently, with his endless arms and legs, let himself fall down too. "Lexidently!" he cried.

The girl started giggling, then laughing, and in the end the three of them laughed so hard that Dimdog stood up in a fright and started barking.

They picked corncobs and ate.

"How did you cure Dimdog?"

"Travelers' secret."

"How come your dogs were sick?"

"Travelers' secret."

"Is everything you do a travelers' secret?"

"It is for a townie."

"What's a townie?"

"You're a townie." She peeled another corncob, teasingly throwing the husks at his head. "Townies' welcome!"

"I had to do it," he said. "My father…" He had to get it out. It had been worrying him.

She nodded. "Fathers are bastards," she said.

She drew on the ground with a stick. Here, and here, and here: a window. There, a door with a stone doorstep. That doorstep was clearly important; she drew it over four times. Small, bigger, biggest. In the center of the clearing, where Dimdog had just been lying, she drew a rectangle. That was going to be the table. No, a round one would be better. It had to be a round table. A chair here, and here, and here, each of them a scratch in the soil. The last chair was real, but sitting on it wasn't really possible, so she stood half-squatting over Charley's chair, her too-large skirt half-covering it. She said that if you squinted, it looked just as if she was really sitting down. She said Charley should screw up his eyes to see it that way, but that Lexidently wasn't able to do that, to see things that weren't there.

"My brother," she said.

Charley had never seen two people so unlike each other.

"Later, I'm going to live in a house with a stone doorstep," she said.

"Later, I'm going to grow tall," said Charley.

For a whole week, whenever he had a chance, he ran down Sjlammbams Sahara to the house of corn and earth. Then they played their game—her game, really. All he did was watch as she swept the make-believe doorstep in front of her house and brought in the imaginary washing. And if the coal (lumps of brown soil) ran out, she'd call out, "Quick, quick, the fire is going out." But she never gave him the chance to find fresh lumps. Instead, she'd push him aside and walk among the rustling cornstalks. At times he could see her face, flushed red and too intense for what was just a game.

She would cover up Lexidently, who'd stretch himself out

on a bed of corncobs, his hand resting on Dimdog's head.

"I am the lady and you are the man," she'd say to Charley. "He is the child and this is our house."

Side by side on their backs, they lay without touching on the corncob bed.

"Where are you going after the summer?" he asked.

"Shush," she said.

"Back again?"

"Travelers' secret."

"Belgium?"

"Shush."

"Belgium?"

"Travelers' secret."

"Farther than Belgium?"

"Yes."

"France?"

"Farther."

"Farther?"

"Much farther away. Now let's go to sleep."

He folded his arms under his head and thought. Imagine being able to just go away. Imagine leaving the town and being able to just go somewhere else!

"Much farther away" were the three loveliest words he could think of.

One afternoon she came without Lexi. He had climbed a tree again, she said, and let himself fall out of it, and now there was blood coming from his ear.

"Shouldn't he see a doctor?" he asked.

She shrugged. "Now you are the child," she said.

He felt himself tensing up. "No."

"You have to," she said.

"You could be the child, couldn't you?"

"You're the smallest. If you don't do it, you can get the heck out of here," she said.

He whistled for Dimdog.

"Stay here," she shouted, furious. "Stay here!" And when he didn't: "I know what they call you! Bottletop. Charley the Bottletop."

"Nienevee!" he shouted back. It was the first offensive name that came into his head, even though it made no sense. Nienevee was what a sulky child was called, and there was nothing sulky about Nienevee, and she certainly wasn't a child. But what had been said was said: "Nienevee from Outside the Walls!"

What happened next was something he would have liked to forget. Three boys—the blacksmith Hermes' son and farmer Kalle's two boys—had lit a fire behind St. Rosa's chapel. They had a skinned rabbit, whose bloody skin they'd carelessly tossed to the ground.

"Bottletop!"

They proudly showed him the rabbit, half raw, half burnt. He didn't know why he started talking about Nienevee. Maybe he was still angry.

They jumped up as one. "Where?"

He was sorry already, but there was no going back. He pointed vaguely.

Their eyes glittered as they took off. "Those bloody travelers need to know their place."

He hoped they wouldn't find her.

They found her.

He hoped they'd only play a joke on her.

It was no joke.

Kalle's youngest son grabbed Nienevee's chair and smashed it.

The blacksmith's son produced the blood-covered rabbit skin.

Nienevee bit a hole in the blacksmith's son's cheek. She kicked Kalle's eldest in the crotch, but then they got a firm hold on her. They pushed her down onto the corncob bed and sat on top of her. She cursed, she kicked, she cried, first out of fury, then out of helplessness.

"Stop it!" Charley shouted. He tried to pull them off, but they easily shoved him aside.

They pulled up her skirt.

Charley heard a terrifying roar. It was a crying scream, as if the cornfield itself was roaring. The next moment, Lexidently was there. He had a bandage around his head, but it was half undone. He had never looked so big. He pushed the first boy off with a single blow. He dragged the second into the cornfield by his hair. Those two couldn't get away fast enough. As for the blacksmith's son, Lexidently pushed his face down into the mud exactly as he'd done to Charley two weeks earlier. Only this time he sat on the boy's head.

"Lexidently!" he shouted. "Lexidently!"

The blacksmith's son's body was shaking. Charley could hear him retching, but Lexidently's big hands wouldn't let go.

"Lexidently!"

"Let go!" shouted Nienevee. "Let go!"

But Lexidently was out of control.

The blacksmith's boy groped around in the soil, trying to get a grip. He clawed into thin air. He growled and twitched, shook and spat, trembled and gurgled. Then his clawing hand relaxed.

A man appeared from among the corn. He grabbed hold of Lexidently and dragged him off the blacksmith's son, who started to recover, panting and retching at the same time. His nose, his eyes, his ears were all full of mud.

"What is going on here?" the man demanded.

"What business is it of yours?" Nienevee wanted to know. Charley held his breath. He had recognized the man as Van Wessum.

"This land belongs to me, my girl," said Van Wessum.

"Land belongs to nobody," said Nienevee.

Van Wessum looked at her thoughtfully. He was a tall, bony man with eyes that moved quickly, like water. It was as though a bit of the ocean had stayed behind in them after his journey across the sea.

"Maybe that's how it was once," he said. "And maybe it will be like that again. But for now, this land belongs to me."

Nienevee looked as if she wanted to say something, but she didn't get the chance.

"I just want to know what's going on," he said sharply.

The blacksmith's son was happy to tell him all about it. How he and some pals just happened to be in the area. They'd heard somebody was stealing corn from the brickworks. They were just going to have a look but were attacked. By at least ten travelers. "Isn't that right, Charley?"

Charley looked at Nienevee, but she clamped her lips

together and said nothing.

Van Wessum looked slowly from one to the other. His glance lingered on Nienevee.

"Good," he said. "I understand."

"We should get the police," said the blacksmith's boy, spitting out a tooth.

"I have a better idea," said Van Wessum. They stared at each other. "What I'd really like to do is to give all of you a good hard kick." He started to take his coat off. "Of course, you could wait for that kick, or…"

That was all they needed. The blacksmith's boy disappeared into the corn to the left. Lexidently, Nienevee, and Charley went to the right.

"That didn't hurt at all," said Nienevee when they stood on Sjlammbams Sahara. She walked away without another word.

The following evening, he waited for her in the cornfield. But she didn't come.

Nor did she the evening after that.

Then, just as suddenly as the travelers had arrived, they disappeared once again. This happened a couple of weeks later, the night after the summer fruit harvest had finished. Now the muddy field was empty, aside from a few horse droppings and a faded, torn piece of cloth that flapped about in a tree.

One afternoon in late autumn, Charley and Dimdog found themselves in Van Wessum's cornfield. It was now covered with stubble. Nothing was left of the house drawn in the dirt. Rain and an early snow had obliterated every trace of it. Only the short, thick post Dimdog had been tied to that summer was still there.

Ask Who Could Set Fire to Water

FIVE YEARS HAD PASSED.

"So," said Nienevee. "So, Bottletop."

She stepped into the workshop. At first, Charley hardly recognized her. She had grown tall and thin, and her copper hair was tied back in a severe knot. Instead of the too-large coat, she wore a jacket whose sleeves were too short, which made her look even taller. But the reckless eyes in the freckled face were the same.

"How's your dog?" she asked.

"Good. And Lexidently?"

"Dead."

That shocked him. Not so much Lexi's having died—that wasn't all that surprising—but the casual way in which she said it.

"How?"

"A tree that was too tall."

He bent over the lathe. When he dared look up again, she had gone.

The next time she came, he was working with Lame Krit. She came in softly, a silhouette against the bright afternoon light outside.

"She's come to see me," Charley said quickly.

Lame Krit obviously didn't recognize her, for he just muttered that Charley should take off the clamps and shuffled off to the back room.

"Okay," Charlie called after him.

"And tell Walraven that the timber has to go back. It's full of knots."

"Okay."

"And when you've finished with those clamps, I'll need two dowels."

"All right."

When Lame Krit reappeared from the back room, he picked up his walking stick and slowly left the workshop.

It was quiet. Church bells sounded in the distance.

"Who said I've come to see you?" she asked.

"I just thought."

They were silent again.

Then she said, "It wasn't your fault."

"What?"

"Those boys in the field. The rabbit."

Typical Nienevee from Outside the Walls. To walk in after five years and—bang—get right on with it. But he was happy that she'd said it.

He had seen the travelers three times since that first summer. They always came in late summer to help with the fruit picking, and they always disappeared again halfway through the autumn. And every time, there was the same trouble. But no more animals were poisoned and Nienevee had never been bothered again. Sometimes the group was larger, at other times smaller. Sometimes they missed a year, but when they came, she was always with them. There was no more time, though, for Nienevee to draw houses in the cornfield. Now she had to pull her own weight.

"How long are you here this time?"

"Are you here all day?"

"Until after the harvest?"

"Do you ever go to the cornfield?"

"Never."

"Me neither," she said. "When do you never go there?"

"I'm not Lexidently," he spluttered a week later when she grabbed him by his shirttail and pulled him into the dense corn. This time there was no open space, so she flattened down a patch. They lay down, shoulder to shoulder. Awkwardly, he lay next to her and stared up at the sky. Of course he had kissed girls before, and the rest he had almost done a few times, too, but Nienevee wasn't a girl. Nienevee was…well, Nienevee.

The creaking of a passing cart sounded in the distance. Somewhere, a blackbird sang.

They lay still. Five minutes, ten, twenty. Clouds floated over them and disappeared again.

He thought of her dark eyes. He thought of her voice. All he could do was think about her because he didn't dare look sideways.

He must have fallen asleep. How that was possible, he didn't know. When he woke up with a start, she had already gotten up and was brushing off her skirt and jacket.

"Are you my girlfriend now?" he asked. He wanted to

sound casual, but he sounded more like a squeaking mouse.

"Ha!"

"So…no?"

"Don't start getting ideas in your head, Bottletop," she said.

He didn't know why she went on seeing him. To be honest, he didn't really know why he went on seeing her, either. You couldn't say she was good looking. She was tall and straight as a stick. Nor could you say she was nice or fun to be with, for all they did was lie on their backs together looking up at the sky.

What he did know was that she was Nienevee from Outside the Walls. That she had come from Much Farther Away and that she would go Much Farther Away again.

"You used to say you were going to live in a house with a stone doorstep."

"You used to say you were going to be tall."

He looked at his short arms and legs, and at his small hands. He just hadn't grown, which happened sometimes.

"Then you wouldn't be my Bottletop anymore," she said.

Had she really said "my" or had he imagined it?

He didn't dare ask.

One day, he took Dimdog along to the field.

"Hello doggie, hello lonely doggie," she said, clapping her hands.

Dimdog wagged her tail and pressed her blunt nose against Nienevee's jacket.

"She remembers you," said Charley.

"I think this is what she remembers," she said, producing a piece of sausage from her jacket pocket.

Snap. Swallow. Gone.

Nienevee was still Nienevee and Dimdog was still Dimdog.

"You've never told me how you saved her," he said. "Or why your dogs were so sick the following day."

She tickled the dog behind her ears. Dimdog sat down, sighing with contentment.

"Travelers' secret, I suppose," he tried.

"Of course."

"Can you really set fire to water?"

"Says who?"

"Everybody. Can you?"

"Sure."

"Give someone kidney stones?"

"Does everybody say so?"

"Yes. So, can you?"

"Of course."

"Curse someone so he dies, or will never have children?"

"A bit harder. But it can be done."

Was he meant to believe her? Her face gave nothing away. He took a deep breath.

"And can you also make somebody better?"

She looked at him, for a second, no more.

"Your old man, I suppose?"

How could she know that?

"Don't make a face," she said. "The first time I saw your father he took such strides, even with that crippled leg, that most people couldn't keep up with him. Now he shuffles along like an old man. You don't need to be a traveler to see he's ill."

"They think it's his bones, but they don't know what exactly. He's getting stiffer all the time. At first it was just his back. Now it's his legs, too." Charley stared straight ahead.

"Hey," Nienevee said softly. "Weren't fathers supposed to be bastards?"

A week later, she gave him a little bundle: a crumpled-up piece of cloth with string around it. There was something inside. Something that felt gritty and smelled a bit musty.

"Give it to him," she said.

"What should he do with it?"

"Nothing."

"Should he eat it?"

She shook her head. "Just give it to him."

"What is it?" he asked.

Nienevee gave the usual answer. "And I'm certainly not doing it for him."

"No."

"I spit on the townspeople. I spit on the whole world if it comes right down to it."

"I know."

"Just so you don't think that's why I'm doing it."

"No."

"Because he doesn't deserve it."

"No."

"And don't you start getting ideas into your head, Bottletop."

"No."

"Can you actually say anything other than no and yes?"

"Thank you."

"Oh, piss off."

Lame Krit was in their tiny kitchen, sitting on the tall chair

Charley had made especially for him. It was the only chair he could still get off without help.

"Here."

"What's this?"

"Something good for you."

"Where'd you get it?"

"It's a present."

"Who from?"

"You have to carry it with you."

"I have to nothing." Lame wheezed, his head flushing red after just those few words.

"Just take it," said Charley.

"Don't make me angry, Bottletop! I can still beat you. With one finger, if necessary." Lame swept his stick over the table. He missed the bundle but hit a cup. It shattered on the tiled floor. "Stiff doesn't mean mad! Do you hear? Do you hear me?"

That night from his bedroom, Charley heard his father rummaging around and cursing. For some time now, Lame Krit had been afraid of going to sleep. He was afraid he would wake up with his whole body stiff as a plank. Afraid he would only be able to move his eyes. Afraid he would die.

"Pick it up," Charley muttered softly. "Please pick it up, old man. Please pick it up."

Three months later, well after Nienevee had left, Lame died. Charley found him. For the first time in a year, he was lying in his own bed, the blanket pulled smooth over him, as if the bed had just been made. In his right hand he held the little bundle. His face was so peaceful that many people at the wake had to look twice before they could recognize him.

Ask Who Built Her a House

———

IT WAS A YEAR after Lame Krit's death, and Dimdog was the first to know. She'd been sniffing about outside, running along Sjlammbams Sahara, through the Putse Gate into the town. She'd waited for the milk cart, peed near the broom-seller's stall, nibbled on a piece of bone that had fallen from the slaughterman's cart. Then she had trotted calmly into the workshop.

At first, Charley didn't notice anything. He heard her nails ticking on the floor while she turned around and around, trying to find the perfect spot. Then she lay down, uttering a contented sigh.

He grinned. "Hello, old girl."

He set the heavy wheel of the lathe in motion and started turning wood. The piercing sound of metal on wood and the wood shavings flying about would chase most dogs away, but not Dimdog. Since Lame Krit's death, she had been allowed to lie in the workshop.

After an hour, Charley wiped the sweat off his forehead and turned around. Only then did he see it. Hanging from

Dimdog's collar was a corncob. His heart missed a beat.

That afternoon, on his way back from the timber merchant, Charley had almost bumped right into her in the market square. But Nienevee wasn't on her own and showed no sign of recognizing him. The woman with the boxer's nose was with her, as well as a third unfamiliar woman. They were at the butcher's, trying to swap pieces of brightly-colored cloth for meat. Charley walked past her without a word, but stopped two stalls farther along. He pretended to listen to the knife-grinder's spiel, but meanwhile kept an eye on her. The butcher made a scandalously low offer. The women spat on the ground, turned around, and disappeared.

"Good riddance to bad rubbish," said the butcher once they were out of earshot.

There was laughter.

"So, Bottletop," said Nienevee that evening. They stood in the shelter of the pass, but Charley felt as if he was standing in the middle of a wide open plain. He grinned down at the tips of his shoes.

"So, Nienevee."

She had changed again. No longer was she straight as a stick. He had noticed that already in the market square. She was still tall, or taller than he, but that wasn't saying much. What he saw was that she had become more beautiful, though he couldn't say exactly how.

"I haven't set fire to water yet," she said.

"Huh?"

"The way you look at me."

He blushed and she laughed, but it didn't sound mocking. Awkward, rather. He felt lucky Dimdog was there because talking about the dog allowed them to keep the conversation going. The things he really wanted to say stayed locked inside. He didn't dare speak them.

"Well," she said.

"Well," he said.

And they went their separate ways.

To calm down, he sharpened the chisels and gouges in the workshop. His small hands worked with great care. He even managed to get the small mortise chisel back in shape and so sharp that its steel sparkled.

The workshop was beginning to look like a storeroom with the new furniture Van Wessum had ordered. There were chairs in a stack. A table top without legs leaned against the wall. A writing desk was still being glued. The double bed was nearly finished.

In the town, they said Van Wessum had always been crazy. Who else would grow corn just for fun? Who else would order new furniture and have a new house designed without having found the woman he wanted to marry? And who, for that matter, would remain a bachelor on his thirty-ninth birthday?

Van Wessum, that's who.

Van Wessum, who had had his palm read across the ocean and had believed ever since that he would marry on his fortieth.

But then, he was rich, wasn't he? And the rich do as they like. The townspeople knew better than to remark on it, since the bricks from his factory meant bread on the table for many in the town.

Charley had never taken much notice of the gossip. Van Wessum might be a bit odd, but he certainly wasn't crazy.

He stared at the furniture.

Was that when he got the idea?

"Still on the road at this late hour?" the gatekeepers remarked when Charley left the town the next evening.

Charley nodded.

It was quite a job getting everything out there without anyone seeing, but God favors lovers. He pushed the cart behind a bush, climbed up the slope, walked into the cornfield, cleared an area, and went back and lugged the whole lot, one piece at a time, into the corn. *I must be crazy*, he thought. *Crazier than Lexidently, dumber than Dimdog.*

As if he had a blueprint in his head, he knew exactly where everything had to go. It took him two hours. Then he sat down and waited.

He heard her coming; heard her breathing; heard her pushing through the corn. She was coming. He felt his back tense; his eyes wouldn't blink. She was coming. Then, she was there. She stepped into the clearing and saw everything. She took a step back, dumbfounded. She swayed, nearly falling.

She saw Nienevee's house. Nienevee's house in the middle of the cornfield, full of real furniture.

Charley had even pushed boards under the chair legs so they wouldn't sink into the ground.

"So you can sit down properly. But don't move too much," he warned.

Nienevee went from chair to chair. She sat at each side of the table. He saw how she held her breath. He felt himself holding his, too.

She liked the bed best.

"Then I would be the lady and you the gentleman," she laughed.

Since when could Nienevee laugh like that?

She stepped into the empty bed, the bed without a mattress, without blankets. And he had to follow, for she kept holding his hand. Nienevee couldn't stop looking. She bent over the footboard, touching the carved figures and lines. She laughed out loud at the little chair that stood in the middle of the carved road.

She touched the waving grain and said she could hear the wind.

"How?" she wanted to know.

And he told her. About chisels and gouges, and how he tapped the wood with his mallet. He explained that force was only a small part of carving, and that guiding each tool in the right direction to the right depth was at least as important. He told her how wood could listen, but also that it could turn against you, even break, if it felt you weren't listening to it. The burin, he said, was his favorite tool. It was small and sharp and allowed him to engrave. Did she see the grain swaying in the wind? The small side towers of the church in the distance? The detail of the stones in the town wall? The chair on the road? All of it had been done with the burin.

It was a warm night, one of the last of that year. They lay in Van Wessum's bed, the dark shadows of the rest of the furniture around them, amidst the rustling corn.

"You can ask me anything," she said.

"Anything?"

"Anything."

He thought. "That little bundle for my father. What was in it?"

"Travelers' secret."

"That's no answer."

She sat up, leaning on her elbows. He could feel her breath.

"Travelers' blood, of course," she said. "The eye of a blind rabbit. Two—"

He put his hand over her mouth, surprising even himself by his boldness.

"I really want to know."

She gave him the Nienevee look. A probing look. Then she said, "Soil."

"Just soil?"

"I didn't say 'just.'"

"What sort of soil?"

"Birth-soil," she said, "From the ground where a traveler is born, we take a handful of soil and wrap it in a bundle. So each traveler will always know where he has come from. They say it helps."

"So…What sort of soil did you give my father?"

"Soil from here, of course, you idiot."

He felt a little disappointed, but at the same time he felt as if a load had fallen from his shoulders.

"And what about Dimdog?"

"What?"

"You saved her, didn't you?"

She said nothing.

"She had poison in her stomach, didn't she?"

She said nothing.

"But I saw with my own eyes how my father put rat poison into the sausage," he said irritably. "You saved her. With a travelers' secret."

"Sometimes a secret isn't what you think," she said.

He kept his mouth shut. Perhaps that would work better.

"Look," she said. In her hand she held a corncob. "What am I holding?"

"A corncob."

"Shut your eyes for a minute."

Obediently, he did as he was told.

"Now open them again."

He opened them again.

"And now," she said. "What am I holding now?"

He stared at her stupidly. "I told you. A corncob."

"Wrong," she said with a giggle.

Nienevee giggling. Nienevee saying a corncob wasn't a corncob. Things had better not get any stranger.

"Look behind you."

He turned around. There lay another corncob.

"There's your corncob," she said.

It slowly dawned on him. "You had two of them."

"Mmm."

"Two corncobs." He looked at her, totally bewildered. "The sausage!"

"Yes."

"There were two sausages?"

For a moment, he was face down in the mud again, with Lexidently's hand pushing him down. For how long? Long enough...

"But where did you get a second sausage from so quickly?"

Nienevee grinned. "I told you it wasn't the first time. After a while, you get to know all kinds of townies' welcomes. We saw you coming, we saw you aiming the sausage. While Lexi lay on top of you, I picked up the second sausage. You didn't notice. In the dark, all sausages look alike."

He still couldn't get it.

"We always keep a sausage handy, Bottletop," she explained patiently. "One without poison. So when another townie comes to poison our dogs, we grab him. You were lucky my father was asleep, because he usually makes the townie eat the sausage. The fake one, I mean. The townie thinks he's very nearly dead, and we tell him we know an antidote but he'll have to pay for it. You would be amazed how generous that makes a townie!"

"But what about your dogs? They were sick, weren't they?"

"Travelers' herbs. Makes anybody violently ill."

"So there are no travelers' secrets? No travelers' curses?"

"Did I say that?"

Charley laughed and laughed. With every laugh, a bit of the mystery disappeared, but at the same time, something else took its place.

That night, he hardly slept. All he could do was think: *Nienevee, Nienevee, Nienevee.*

Ask Who Waited

———

CHARLEY KEPT IT UP for three nights. At nightfall, he'd load up his cart, ride to the cornfield, and unload everything. And early in the morning, as soon as the town gates were opened, he'd ride back home. It was idiotic, it was insane, but he did it anyway.

"Late night, Bottletop?" said the guard.

"Special order," said Charley. "Rich folk. You know how it is."

Charley and Nienevee talked less and less. There was no need to talk. There were other things for them to do that were very much like talking.

On the third night, she changed. The night sky was between black and dark blue. Nienevee cried for Lexidently. Awkwardly, gently, Charlie patted her head.

"I'm not your dog," she said angrily. She dried her tears roughly and promptly started sobbing again.

"What are you crying about now?" he asked.

"About leaving," she said. And then, half-laughing, half-crying, she added, "Can you imagine? A traveler who's homesick?"

"What about your birth-soil?"

"You shouldn't believe everything I say."

"So it's not true?"

"Not everything that's true is right." Then, after a long silence, she said, "If you ever tell anyone, I'll murder you." And when it grew light, "Only when we lie under a stone slab with our name on it can we be sure we're going to stay where we are."

"As long as I can lie there with you," said Charley.

"Promise."

"But you'll have to stop crying," said Charley.

"Fine," said Nienevee.

"And be my girl," said Charley. The words sounded just right. A bit casual, as if they really didn't matter much to him at all.

"Fine," she said again.

Sometimes words could work wonders.

"I have a plan," said Charley.

Actually, it was more of a wish than a plan. He'd had the idea in his head for a long time.

"Let's go away together. Away from the town, away from the travelers. Somewhere else is always better."

"Don't be too sure of that."

"Do you have a better plan?"

She didn't.

"Aren't you willing?" he asked. "Are you afraid of what people will think?"

"I spit on the townspeople," she said calmly. "I spit on the travelers. I spit on the whole world if it comes right down to it. But I don't know if you're really willing."

He was angry, offended, so he turned his back on her.

"All right then," she said.

She was going to wait for him by the blackened oak. They were going to set out from there. At night. And he was absolutely certain that this was what he wanted. He was certain this was what he had always wanted. To go away—much farther away.

Until the moment when he pulled the door of the workshop shut behind him. Until he walked out through the gate and left the town behind him.

Then, suddenly, everything changed.

He walked, stopped, walked on, stopped again.

He felt the town walls behind him. He felt the wind blowing free.

He broke into a sweat. He turned around, ran, and just managed to get through the gate before the guards pulled it, creaking, shut.

Nienevee ignored him for a month.

"You have to be certain it's what you want," she said later, furiously. "I need to be certain it's what you want to do. If we go away, there's no way back for me. I'll be dead to the travelers."

He swore it was what he wanted most. He said he'd gotten scared and panicked, but he was very, very sorry. She had to believe him. She really, really had to believe him.

Charley bought a cart and horse to carry his tools and

equipment.

"Are you expanding?" asked old Nol, who still ran the bar.

"Working hard?" asked Farmer Kalle. "We hardly ever see you nowadays."

If Charley had been paying more attention, he would have noticed the look those two exchanged.

And so it was that on the very evening that Nienevee secretly packed up some clothes, waited for the other travelers to go to sleep, and kept glancing toward Sjlammbams Sahara, Charley had a visit from Nol, farmer Kalle, and their sons.

"Can you spare us a few lumps of coal, Charley?"

Charley nodded. They followed him. Four men and one coal scuttle.

Seems like a lot of men for a little bit of coal, Charley thought briefly. But then he let it go. He unlocked the workshop and lit the kerosene lantern. He kept the flame low so it would be less obvious that the workshop was nearly empty. He had loaded as much as possible onto the cart, leaving only the lathe. A dead pity, but it was just too heavy.

"Been tidying up?" said one of the men.

He mumbled something about good riddance and they laughed again.

He opened the coal shed.

"Help yourselves," he said.

"Could you get it for us?" said Kalle's son, pointing at the very low door. "It's easier for someone your size."

Charley took the coal scuttle and stepped into the shed.

The door slammed shut.

"It's for your own good," they said, bolting the door. "Give some thought to Lame Krit. He'd be turning over in his grave if he knew."

"Knew what?"

"Do you think the town is blind? Do think we're stupid? All those trips you've been making down Sjlammbams Sahara with your cart full of furniture? Furniture for Van Wessum, note. We're not stupid."

"Let me out."

"Only when you can see sense."

"But I can see sense. I've never seen better sense than now. I'm leaving."

"With that traveler girl? Not likely. If you go off with that wench, the travelers will be furious. What do you think will happen next? They'll find somebody to blame. We don't want to be the ones who are cursed."

"There is no such thing as curses."

The men looked at each other and turned around together. Charley heard them walk away. He heard the gate to the courtyard shut and the key turn in the lock. Now no one would be able to hear him, but he shouted himself hoarse all the same.

And all the while, he thought of Nienevee.

Nienevee, who now stood waiting for him with all her things. Nienevee, who had doubted if he really wanted to go. Nienevee, who could never go back.

Later, much later, he heard that she had waited all night. Farmer Kalle had seen it all. He'd seen the travelers waiting for her and their travelers' farewell, which could not be misunderstood. And it was Van Wessum, the brick-factory owner, who had found her the next morning, in the dip in the hillside, all alone, pale, and grim-faced.

The same Van Wessum who six years earlier had agreed that once upon a time the land had belonged to no one, and that it might be like that again some day, but not yet.

It was Van Wessum who found her, who first offered her a job as a servant, and who, less than a year later, asked her to marry him. Exactly on his fortieth birthday.

And she said yes, on one condition.

"Have you heard?" they said in the town. "Have you heard what that traveler woman has wrangled this time? She's going to get a new house. Not here, but at the end of the world! She says she spits on the townspeople, on the travelers, and on the whole world if it comes right down to it. She says she'll show us, too. Three guesses how!"

PART THREE
The Wanderer of
Sjlammbams Sahara

Townies' Welcome

THE MAGIC OF THAT night was fast disappearing.

Through the kitchen window, I watched the black sky turn gray. The moonlight faded and the glowing sand of Sjlammbams Sahara was beige and ordinary once again. In an hour or so, it would be day.

Our brothers stretched and slapped each other's faces teasingly. "Stay awake! Stay awake!"

Had we really stayed up all night? In one way it felt as if we'd only just sat down, as if we'd brought Oompah Hatsi inside only a minute ago. At the same time, it felt as though I'd been there for centuries. With my heart thumping, I had crept along with Charley. I had seen Nienevee dancing in the cornfield with the chair in her arms, and I'd felt what it was like when her chair sank into the soft earth when she sat down. I had desperately hoped she would go away with Charley. And I had seen her sitting in the dip in the hillside, abandoned by everyone.

I had cried.

"Nienevee had a house built on the very spot where, in the past, the travelers were not allowed to stay," said Oma Mei. "And she called it Townies' Welcome." She got up slowly and filled the kettle. "She had the name made out of cast iron. And the day she married Van Wessum, she put it up above the front door so everyone could see it."

"Above the front door?" wondered Muulke.

"Yes."

"So those four holes are where it was attached?"

Oma Mei nodded.

"So no bullet holes?"

Strangely enough, Muulke didn't look disappointed.

"What happened after that?" I asked.

Oma Mei shrugged. "Nothing. She and Van Wessum lived in the house until they died."

"Are they buried here?"

"No, in the old cemetery."

"And Charley?"

Oma Mei got up and walked toward the living room. "Nobody knows."

Softly, she opened the sliding door. We could hear Oompah Hatsi snoring. Our grandmother put a scoop of *sjlamm* into the Belgian potbellied stove and put the kettle on. Despite the burning stove, it was chill and damp in the house. I shivered and pulled my sweater tight around me. Oma Mei came back into the kitchen and shut the door.

"A cannon shot wouldn't wake that one," she said.

"That's all well and good," said Eet. "But what in God's name does that whole story have to do with Oompah?"

Piet, Sjeer, and Krit nodded to show they were puzzled, too. It was strange to realize that our brothers could do sums in their heads to the second decimal point, and they could see if a window that was to become a door was just a fraction off. But they still couldn't see some other, perfectly obvious things. "Boys aren't girls and girls aren't boys," Oma Mei had often said, and I was beginning to see what she meant.

"Do you really not see it?" asked Oma Mei.

Our brothers looked annoyed.

"He is Nienevee and Charley's son," I said.

"*Kwatsj!*" they shouted. They tapped their foreheads, huffed and puffed indignantly, and then tiptoed off to have a look at the snoring button-chewer.

"Are his hands small like a dressmaker's?" we asked them softly. "And, apart from gray, is his beard the color of copper?"

They stood there and let it all sink in. Oompah Hatsi, the button-chewer, the son of Charley Bottletop and Nienevee from Outside the Walls?

"*Kwatsj!* Oh well ...What does it matter, really..."
They came back into the kitchen, stretched, cracked their knuckles, and tried to outdo each other with stories about madmen and madhouses.

"But what did Charley do after Nienevee had accepted Van Wessum's proposal?" Dad asked with a yawn.

"He left," replied Oma Mei. "When he heard that Nienevee had accepted Van Wessum, he left, leaving all of his belongings behind, including the furniture that Van Wessum had ordered, but never collected. All of it had been carefully stacked and wrapped in rags, and that's how it was moved. Four large cartloads. Everything was carefully arranged and displayed in the house. The dining-room chairs, the armchairs, the writing desk. Every piece had been made exactly as Van Wessum had ordered. Everything…"

Muulke and I looked at each other.

"…except the bed," I said.

"He'd made that look like a tombstone," Muulke exclaimed.

Oma Mei nodded.

"And those dates?" I asked.

"1863 was the year they met," said Oma Mei. "And in 1870, Nienevee married Van Wessum."

"But why are those dates there together?" asked Muulke. "And why did he make the headboard like like a tombstone?"

We were silent for a while.

"Because their love lived for such a short time."

We looked at our grandmother but realized instantly that it wasn't she who had given that answer. The voice had come from the passage.

Wrapped in a blanket, Jess sat halfway up the stairs, leaning against the railing, her arms around the supports.

"Have you been sitting there all this time?" asked Oma Mei, more worried than angry.

Jess nodded sleepily.

"Take her upstairs immediately," said Oma Mei.

Dad lifted her up. "You'll have to put on a bit of weight, little bird. One of these days you'll be blown away."

Jess opened her eyes and made a final effort to stay awake. "Love lived for such a short time," she said once more. Her voice sounded terribly sad. "First he loved her, and then he didn't any more. She killed his love. And that's why the bed had to be like a grave. Isn't it sad?"

Our brothers and Muulke went back into the kitchen. From the passage, I could hear them moving their chairs around and pouring coffee. Suddenly, I realized how tired I was.

Oma Mei was still in the passage, staring at the stairs. Her back was broad and a bit rounded, and she stood as if she was leaning into an invisible storm. "Let's hope you can find rest now," she said. Her voice sounded thoughtful, almost pleading.

"Who?" I asked. "Oompah?"

She turned around abruptly. I caught just a glimpse of her swivel-eye, fluttering wildly, before she hurriedly pressed it shut with her finger.

"Yes, of course," she said. "Who else?"

Then she chased Muulke and me upstairs.

Ten Open Arms

AND SO THE HOUSE got another pair of arms.

"It should really be called Ten Open Arms now," said Muulke.

"Ten Poor Arms," Oma Mei grumbled. "Ten poorer than poor arms."

As if she'd had nothing to do with the button-chewer coming to live with us. "What else can we do?" she had exclaimed. We were lying with our ears flat to the crack in the floor of our bedroom. "He can't possibly look after himself, that's obvious. And I really can't deliver the poor man to the Ursuline Sisters or the Franciscan Brothers. Or send him back to the home. Don't you see how crazy that made him?"

"He might be dangerous," said Dad, but we could hear from his tone that he only said it to wind up Oma Mei.

"Oh, come on," said Oma Mei. "That man is only a danger to buttons. He can sleep in the workshop. In a way, it's his home."

"There's plenty of room in the attic, too," said Dad.

"Don't even think about it. We've called down enough

misfortune on ourselves." We heard her sigh. "So for God's sake," she said, as if she still had to convince herself. "Only if he becomes a problem."

But Oompah had a deep respect for her and she scolded him the same as everybody else. "Sit up straight. Are you a bag of coal? Wash your hands. You're not to come to the table like that. You can keep that growling for the fair. They might even pay you for it."

But she looked after his burns every day, and when Oompah ripped his worn trousers one morning, she sent Piet and Krit up to the attic and had them bring down a wooden box full of mothballs and layers of tissue paper. In among those lay our grandfather's carefully folded, barely creased Sunday clothes. And though they were a lot less elegant than the supervisor's clothes in the photo of Opa Pei and his workmen and didn't include a felt hat or a silk vest, they still were remarkably stylish.

"Are you giving him those?" Dad sounded surprised.

"Do I look like the Good Samaritan?" Oma Mei snapped. "He can borrow them. And he'll have to do his own alterations. He's better at that than I am."

"It's only family she talks to like that, Oompah," said Muulke.

A little while later, the button-chewer was sitting on an old chair in front of our house with his mouth full of pins, utterly content. Snip went his scissors.

Whether Oompah actually slept in the workshop, we didn't know. When Dad and our brothers went there in the mornings, they always found the door that used to be a window ajar. He only came into the house for meals, obviously ill at ease, and always made himself scarce right after he'd eaten. When we wondered about that, Oma Mei said there was nothing surprising about it.

"But it's his house, isn't it?" I said.

Oma Mei's face looked grim. "That may be, but it was never his home."

We waited.

"He was only born here," she said.

"What do you mean?"

"That's easy enough to figure!" she exclaimed. "He was Charley's child. Do you really think Van Wessum would accept a child that wasn't his?"

"How horribly mean!" Jess cried out.

"There's nothing mean about it," Oma Mei said curtly. "It just wasn't possible. As soon as the baby was born, Van Wessum took him to the orphanage."

"Did Nienevee agree?" I asked.

"What else could she do? She had been disowned by the travelers. And the townspeople didn't want her, either. Van Wessum allowed her to visit Oompah in the orphanage for an hour once a month. Later on, he could visit her here, but Oompah never set foot inside this house. He always had to wait on the doorstep for her to come outside. And then they walked along Sjlammbams Sahara until the hour was over."

"Poor, poor Oompah," said Jess, her eyes filling with tears.

Was it because of that story? Or because Oompah, dressed in our grandfather's clothes, suddenly looked much less like a tramp? At any rate, Jess seemed to be much less scared of the button-chewer. She no longer ran off when he approached. And one day, when Oompah became restless during a meal and Oma Mei sent him outside, she went after him with his plate.

It was Saturday and Muulke and I were scrubbing the floor when Dad came in with his overcoat still on. He sat down on one chair, then on another. He stirred the fire in the stove, whistled an unrecognizable tune, and kept looking around all the while.

"Is she here?" he asked.

Muulke and I looked at each other.

"Oma Mei is in the vegetable garden," I said.

"Aha," said Dad. He opened his mouth, then shut it again.

"What's the matter?" asked Muulke.

"Oh, nothing, *leeveke*," said Dad. He took a quick look behind the couch, as if he expected our grandmother to be hiding there. "Well, practically nothing."

We waited.

"You haven't seen a, uh, a letter somewhere, have you?"

"A letter?" Muulke echoed.

I started to blush immediately, but Muulke blinked twice and asked calmly what sort of a letter he was talking about.

"Oh well, um," said Dad, flushing bright red in his turn. "Uh...one from the bank."

"Nothing important, I hope?" said Muulke airily.

"No, no, don't be silly," said Dad. "Not really... just a bit." He got that helpless look on his face that made him look like more of an older brother than a father, and a not-much-older brother at that. I wanted to cover my ears with my hands but managed not to.

"What's the matter, then?" I asked.

He beckoned for us to come closer.

"I've borrowed a little bit of money." He put a finger to his lips. "And, well, you know what banks are like."

I didn't understand just what he meant by that, but I understood enough to know that the next disaster was lurking around the corner.

"Does Oma Mei know about this?" I asked, against my better judgment.

"Oh, she gets worried so easily," Dad said casually. "So I thought we needn't tell her yet." He was silent for a little while, and then said, "So, you're absolutely sure you haven't seen that letter?"

He looked straight at me, and I felt my cheeks still burning. Then, he winked, and I knew that he knew, too.

"No," we said.

"So it can't suddenly turn up?"

Muulke and I shook our heads.

"Absolutely sure?"

I thought of the torn-up letter whose bits had been blown all over the place.

"Absolutely sure," I said firmly.

Dad grinned broadly. "Excellent, excellent," he said, and he went outside whistling.

Life went on. We went to school and when we got home, we did our chores around the house.

Dad bought a bale of ready-to-use filler from a new tobacco grower in Tegelen who had only recently gone into business. He and our brothers made five misshapen cigars and lit them. A penetrating smell of sweaty feet filled our house. Dad still insisted that a bargain was a bargain, but less than five seconds later the five of them were in the garden throwing up.

"It wouldn't be the first time," Nol said later, "that someone picked up a case of poisoning from an amateur like that."

"You could have told me a bit sooner," said Dad, still pale as death and sweating.

"I did," said Nol. "But, as usual, you weren't listening."

Life went on as if nothing had happened.

A Homesick Saint

ON THE FIRST MONDAY in June, the boys from the technical school came into our classroom with their teacher. Each of them was carrying a metal frame that looked similar to Jess's straightener, only the slats were metal and were attached to the front as well as to the back.

"Right on time," said Sister Angelica.

The boys stood in a tight group. They hardly dared look up.

We stared at them. We didn't often get to see so many boys at once.

In turn, each of us had to stand up, collect one of the frames, curtsey, and sit back down. Then the boys disappeared.

"Saint Rosa, Saint Rosa," the girls whispered excitedly.

"No whispering," said Sister Angelica. "No need to turn it into a shambles." But her face was flushed with excitement, too.

"Is it for Saint Rosa?"

"Put your hand up first, child."

"Is it for Saint Rosa?"

Sister Angelica beamed.

"Are we getting new wings, Sister?"

Her smile became even broader. "You girls are going to be the loveliest angels ever," she said.

On the back of each frame were four hinges. Fretwork wings would be attached to those. Over the next two months, we were going to make the wings in our needlework classes. First, we would take old sheets from the hospital. Then, one by one, we would sew chicken and pigeon feathers onto the sheets.

"It's going to be wonderful. You'll see," said Sister Angelica.

Then she brought out the moth-eaten map of South America and hung it up on the door. She unrolled it and pointed out the city of Lima, from where Saint Rosa, the patron saint of our town, had come. Then she showed us on the lumpy old globe how great the distance was between Saint Rosa's city and our town.

"Saints get homesick, too," she said, her eyes shining with emotion. "So I want you all to do your very best."

"*Miljaar!*" Muulke cursed when we were walking home. "Chicken feathers! And all done in stupid cross-stitch!" She swished a branch around furiously.

"Watch out," I said. "You'll poke somebody's eye out."

Muulke had always disliked needlework. At our old school, we had never had to use a needle and thread. There had been a Sister for that once, but she had died under the hooves of the butcher's runaway horse. And the Franciscan Brothers couldn't do it all. The only thing they had was an old wood-turning lathe with a foot pedal. Muulke had been the only girl who had managed to get permission to join the boys' woodworking class.

"*Miljaar!*" Muulke said again.

"Do you think I'll be allowed to be in it?" Jess asked.

I thought of the metal frames, and about the wings of wood, old sheets, and feathers.

"We'll ask," I said.

"Can you ask for me?"

"You can do it yourself."

"But you'll do it better," pleaded Jess.

Of course, it turned into a drama. Weeping with fury, Jess stormed out of the kitchen even before Oma Mei had finished speaking. Our grandmother pressed her lips together and cut the bread to shreds, and when I tried to go after Jess, she snapped at me to stay in my seat till after the meal.

"She'll have to get used to the idea that she can't do everything with that wreckbone," she exclaimed, adding that it wasn't for nothing that the words "heart" and "hard" sounded so similar. And when everybody kept silent, she continued, "Do I always have to do everything? Does it always have to be me who's the ogre around here?"

She looked straight at Dad, but he looked up at the clock and was suddenly in a great hurry.

"It's not fair," Jess sobbed.

We found her near Mr. Wetsels' shed. She wiped away her tears and angrily picked at the threadbare burlap that hung in the doorway.

"I want to be an angel, too."

"You can, can't you?" I said.

"You can walk with us without wings, can't you?" said Muulke.

"What's that supposed to mean?"

We were silent. She was right. Who had ever heard of an angel without wings?

"Then Muulke and I will go without wings, too," I said.

"Yes," shouted Muulke, who took up the idea immediately, because then she wouldn't have to do any needlework at all. "Then we'll all look exactly the same!"

"We're not at all exactly the same," Jess snapped. "You're allowed anything you want. I'm not allowed anything. I'm never allowed to do anything."

"Oh, come on," said Muulke.

"Get lost," said Jess.

"Get lost yourself." Muulke walked off.

I held out my arm, but Jess stayed where she was.

I walked back through the fields. It was a dull, gray day. Nine Open Arms looked more dismal than ever with its sagging roof, different color tiles, cracked walls, and the holes above the door where the Townies' Welcome sign had once hung.

And then it happened.

One moment, my thoughts were focused on Jess. The next, it was as if something inside me had shifted. First there was a vague feeling of uneasiness, and then, suddenly, without any reason, I thought, *Something is wrong. Something is very wrong with this house.*

I have no idea where that thought came from, but it came, strong and unmistakable, and as real as a grain of barley in a summer shoe.

Restless

_____

I WAS WALKING ALONG Sjlammbams Sahara with Muulke and Jess. We were on our way to school, and it was late. We tried to run, but no matter how hard we tried, we couldn't make any progress. The wind was too strong. Around us, trees were being blown over with a sharp, crackling sound. Jess shouted that she wanted to take off her straightener. I tried to stop her, but Muulke started tickling me, and suddenly Jess turned into a letter that tore into small pieces in my hands. I desperately tried to keep her with me, but she blew through my fingers. I shouted that she mustn't go away. I knew something terrible was going to happen, but Jess was blown farther and farther away.

Then, suddenly, I was standing in front of Nine Open Arms. A small boy was sitting in front of our door looking curiously at me. I told him to say something, that I couldn't simply guess what he wanted, but he just kept looking at me. I slapped him, and he burst into tears.

I ran to the cemetery but found that the hedge had grown wildly dense. I ran and ran, but couldn't get any farther. The branches and leaves wrapped around me more and more tightly. Above me hung Oma Mei's head, huge, like an angry sun. Twigs got into my mouth and nose. I wanted to scream, but couldn't make a sound. Opa Pei was there, too, in his smart felt hat and silk vest. He and the workers laughed uproariously as Oompah Hatsi shouted, "Fing, Jess, Muu-huuhuulke, look carefully, look carefully!"

I gasped for breath. The gleaming eyes of my sisters floated above me. It was still dark, but no longer night.

"What's the matter with you?" asked Jess.

My throat felt powder-dry. My back was wet with sweat.

"A nightmare," Muulke grinned.

Jess didn't believe a word of it. "Fing never has nightmares," she said. "Fing, you never have nightmares, do you?"

"I was just lying the wrong way," I said.

But the following night, I was running down Sjlammbams Sahara once again. This time the letter was still in one piece, but I knew I had to deliver it very quickly or something terrible would happen. I ran and ran and ran, but couldn't find the house anywhere.

"You have to look," Oompah Hatsi shouted again, putting one cigar after the other into his mouth and eating them. "Look carefully!"

In a panic, I hurled myself through the hedge, which suddenly was yards thick, its branches burning. On the other side sat Oma Mei, madly scrubbing the nameless grave. The soft soap foamed like whipped milk. I slipped and fell, and fell again. Once again, my grandfather couldn't stop laughing. He was bent over, crushing his felt hat in his hand.

"What's wrong?" Muulke asked softly. My nightgown hung over a chair, soaked with sweat. I had put on a fresh one. It was the third night in a row of nightmares.

"Nothing's wrong," I said.

"You're acting weirdly," said Muulke.

I was silent.

"…and you seem miserable."

What could I say? I didn't know what was wrong…If anything was wrong. All I knew was that I couldn't shake a feeling of restlessness. It nagged at my stomach during the day and troubled my dreams at night.

"There's something wrong," I said.

"What?"

"That's the problem, I don't know."

I could hear how dumb that sounded. I searched for words, for something to hang on to. I tried to remember when this feeling had first begun. Was it when I had stood outside the house? Or had it come before that? Suddenly, I knew. "Do you remember when Jess sat on the stairs eavesdropping?"

"Yes."

"Oma Mei said, 'Let's hope you can find rest now.'"

"Let's hope you can find rest now?"

"That's strange, isn't it?"

Muulke was silent.

"And her swivel-eye was fluttering."

"It flutters all the time."

"It was like she was talking to somebody," I insisted. "But no one else was there besides us. When I asked if she meant Oompah she said yes."

"That makes sense, doesn't it?" said Muulke. "Oompah was homeless but now has a roof over his head, so he's found rest, right?"

I looked at Muulke. Where was the Muulke of the tragical tragedies? The Muulke who suspected neighbors of being jewel thieves? Who knew for a fact that a showman with a hairy back was a werewolf? Hearing her now was like listening to myself. As if, by some bizarre magic, I had crawled into her skin and she into mine.

"What about the nameless grave?" I asked.

"What about it?"

"I think it's Charley's."

"Where did you get that idea from?"

"I just think so."

"*Kwatsj*," Muulke yawned. "Charley went away and never came back. That's what Oma said, isn't it?"

"So whose is it?" I asked. "And why is there such a huge crack in the stone?"

"Perhaps a tree blew over one day."

I took a deep breath. It took all of my courage to say what I wanted to say. Especially since I wasn't at all sure I was right.

"I think something bad happened," I said. "And I think Oma Mei had something to do with it."

"Oma Mei? Why would you think that?"

"Then why does she scrub that grave in the middle of the night?"

Muulke yawned. "Maybe you dreamt it."

"How can you say that?" I cried.

Jess groaned. Frowning, she rubbed her hand over her eyes. We were silent. The wind rattled the roof tiles. We waited until her breathing was regular again.

"How can you say a thing like that?" I whispered.

"You said it yourself," Muulke whispered back. "When we were sitting on the front fence you said, 'I may have dreamt it.' Well, perhaps that's how it was."

"But I didn't mean it like that."

"Then why did you say it?"

"I thought you wouldn't believe me."

She grinned. I saw her teeth glittering in the dark, and when she spoke her voice was full of insufferable triumph. "If I didn't know better, I would think you were thinking of a tragical tragedy."

Why was I so angry? It had happened a thousand times before—Muulke driving everyone crazy with her stories of curses and murders, but as soon as anybody else started seeing the world through her eyes, she lost interest.

It had happened so often before that it could only happen again and again. Some things never change.

I was going to have to sort it out myself.

The Order

ON SATURDAY AFTERNOON, OMA Mei heard that there was a sale on meat, so she sent me off to get some. People had already crowded around the butcher's cart in the market square. I got there just soon enough; the people behind me were wasting their time. There was a lot of pushing, complaining, and cursing. To be on the safe side, I pushed the meat, wrapped in old newspapers, to the bottom of my basket and kept a tight hold on it.

I can't quite remember when I got the idea. But instead of walking toward Put Street and home, I walked in the opposite direction—past our school, along the cobbled street where the doctor lived, and then across the town wall, until I was just outside the old center of the town.

The cemetery gate was old and rusty and squeaked solemnly when I opened it. There were no carefully laid-out paths here, only an untidy path, worn down by visitors, through the knee-high grass.

The gravestones of the old cemetery lay in tight circles around a small chapel. It was so crowded that some of the tombstones had been cemented into the outer wall.

It wasn't all that hard to find what I was looking for. It was the only grave made of bricks. It looked straight and angular compared to the rounded shapes of the other graves. It had crenellations, as if it were a little castle. On each corner stood a vase made from bricks, but judging from the thick layer of moss that had grown over them, it must have been a long time since they contained flowers.

HENDRIKUS THEODOOR VAN WESSUM

JANUARY 31, 1830–OCTOBER 20, 1902

Underneath that was a name I didn't recognize—a name I've never been able to remember because it seemed to have so little to do with the girl who built houses in the cornfield. But as soon as I looked at the dates accompanying that name, I knew it was Nienevee.

I stood in front of the brick grave unable to take my eyes off it. Like a math problem with the wrong answer, I knew something somewhere wasn't right, but I couldn't for the life of me work out what.

"Tell me," I muttered. "Please tell me."

But apart from the squeaking of the gate in the wind, there was only silence.

When I got home, our brothers were sitting in the kitchen, straddling the chairs back-to-front. They were leaning their stomachs against the chair backs and Oma Mei wasn't saying anything about it! Or about the fact that they were smoking and dropping cigar ash on the table. They looked very pleased with themselves.

"We've got one," said Piet.

"An order," said Eet.

"For five thousand," said Sjeer.

"To be ready by Saint Rosa's Day," said Krit.

They exhaled together, four mouths open too wide for the tiny bit of smoke they'd managed to suck out of the better-luck-next-time cigars.

On Saint Rosa's Day, the shopkeepers wanted to present gifts to their customers, like always. Originally, it was going to be small bottles of liquor, but the distiller had gone bankrupt, so at the eleventh hour the shopkeepers had decided on cigars instead. They ordered one hundred thousand cigars and the current cigar kings couldn't manage that many on such short notice on top of their other orders. Not even the mechanized cigar emperor could handle it.

"Nol must have something to do with it," was Oma Mei's opinion as she poured coffee.

"It's just that we make the very best cigars anyone has ever tasted," said our brothers.

"Just that," Oma Mei scoffed.

"But…" Jess and Muulke said together.

"No buts," they said. "What does Dad always say?"

Silence.

"Dad?" Our brothers spoke together, hoping to get his attention.

But Dad only looked up absent-mindedly. "What?"

"Believe first, then see, right?"

"Yes, yes," said Dad, still distracted. "Sure thing."

"While I think of it, said Piet, before he and our other brothers went and locked themselves away in the workshop once again, "the cushion Dad always sits on is missing again, and Oma Mei can't find her soup ladle."

"I'll go," I said. "I've got to get water anyway."

Even though Oompah no longer lived in the hedge and had a roof over his head, our grandfather's clothes, and Oma Mei's stern care, that didn't mean he had become even slightly more normal. He still only answered with his little scissors, and he still pilfered constantly. Oma Mei had given him a hard time about it on a few occasions, but it hadn't made much of a difference. And strangely enough, nobody got too worked up about it, either. Whenever people in the town missed something, they just dropped by to collect it. At least twice a week, somebody would walk the length of our long road with a recovered frying pan, a box of cutlery, sheets, dust cloths, or cushions.

I pushed the carriage to the pump. Then I searched the hedge. By now I had worked out where to look, and soon enough I spotted the edge of a large burlap sack among the branches.

As I emptied the sack, I heard a rustling in the passage and imagined that I saw a head disappear.

"You'll have to stop this, Oompah!" I called. "This isn't funny anymore."

I snatched Dad's cushion out of the sack, then our soup ladle. I found two unfamiliar eggcups and a brand new cast-iron pan as well.

The nameless grave looked deserted. I no longer smelled soap, but the stone slab was still free of ivy and looked neat and tidy. Was Oma Mei still scrubbing it?

For a moment I thought about asking her. I would just go up to her...I would...I would...

Kwatsj. I wasn't brave enough, and even if I was, it would be unthinkable for Oma Mei to simply give an answer. Instead, she'd want to know what in the world I thought I was doing out there in the middle of the night. And I wouldn't be able to lie. I'd want to, but I wouldn't be able to. And if she found out about the letter from the bank, if she found out that Dad had borrowed money again, then the fat would really be in the fire.

Even if the Crocodile hadn't moved since Jess had discovered it upright in its cover in our grandmother's bedroom, it still wasn't safely under her bed. And it wouldn't take much to…

A powerless fury surged up inside me. I kicked the stone. "Bug off, whoever you are," I said. "And leave us in peace."

The day of the procession was rapidly approaching. The efforts to turn better-luck-next-time cigars into proper cigars became more and more frantic. Our brothers showed us the results every evening when they placed each cigar between two rulers.

"I reckon these rulers aren't straight," Piet complained.

"That's why these cigars seem less straight than they really are," said Eet.

"This one's getting pretty close to being straight, don't you think, Eet?"

"At least it's a lot less bent, Sjeer."

We tried to improve the cigars by looking at them, and though we thought they had become a little less misshapen, they still didn't look much like the cigar kings' cigars, not to mention the cigar emperor's.

Over the next few days, we found Dad in the passage, in the kitchen, and by the gate—everywhere except the workshop.

"Is everything going all right?" we would shout at the living room wall.

"Well enough," our brothers would shout back.

We'd inquire how many cigars they'd made so far.

They'd shout back that it wasn't about quantity but quality.

We weren't allowed to go in, and they even kept the door locked, so after three days we finally peered in through the window that had always been a window and saw the cigars.

"Quite a stack," said Muulke.

"A little stack," said Jess.

"How many?" I asked.

"A hundred," Muulke guessed.

"Fifty at the most," said Jess. She looked at me. "How much is five thousand minus fifty?"

"Far too much," I said.

We calculated till our heads spun. Fifty cigars in three days: that was sixteen and some a day. That times seven made a hundred and something. And that times the number of weeks till the Saint Rosa's Day procession made…made…

"Where are our brothers when we need them?" said Muulke.

"Anyway, at this rate they'll never get to five thousand," wailed Jess.

"And we're not even talking about how to turn better-luck-next-time cigars into real cigars."

That night, I was pursued by a man from the Rotterdam Banking Society. He rode after me on a tiny little bicycle, shouting, "The opposite of worrying, the opposite of worrying!" Then it started raining cigars—bent, thick, hollow, cracked, useless cigars. They fell on my head and hurt. I started digging a hole to hide in, but suddenly two pale hands reached up from the black soil. They grabbed me and pulled me down into the ground. Soil got into my mouth, my nose, my eyes. Everything went black.

The Virgin Mary in an Armchair

WHEN WE WALKED INTO the schoolyard, I could tell right away that something was going on.

"Why are they staring at us?" asked Jess.

"Who's staring?" Muulke said.

"Everybody," said Jess.

"*Kwatsj, sjiethoes*," said Muulke.

But it wasn't nonsense.

Just before we had to line up, a girl came up to Muulke and me. I vaguely knew her. She was in her final year.

"Is it true that Jess is going to be the Virgin Mary?" she asked.

We looked at each other.

"Says who?" asked Muulke.

"Everybody," said the girl. She looked at us darkly. "I would look out if I were you."

"Look out? What for?" Muulke shot back.

The bell rang.

The day after Oma Mei had said it was high time Jess got used to the fact that she couldn't do everything, and it wasn't for nothing that "heart" and "hard" sounded so similar, she had gone to visit the headmistress, her old school friend.

"The Sisters still need a Virgin Mary," Oma Mei had said when she returned.

"What does that Virgin Mary have to do?" Jess had asked.

"I don't know about the other Virgin Marys," Oma Mei had replied, "but you'll have to sit in an armchair."

As far as we knew, a Virgin Mary in an armchair had never been part of the procession before. Marys usually stood in a papier-mâché grotto on a float, holding a bundle of rags in their arms, or they had to kneel for two hours in front of a fretwork mountain landscape. They always wore an iron hoop around their waist that was attached to the float so they wouldn't fall off.

That hoop, and Jess having to stand or kneel throughout the procession, were out of the question. So Oma Mei had suggested that an armchair with a good straight back could work, and a grotto could easily be built around that.

I suspected that Jess didn't really like the idea.

"The doctor told me there are straighteners that don't squeak," Jess had said. "They have elastic straps instead of leather ones with buckles."

"That's all very well, but with the debts we have we can't even afford to buy a shoe lace, let alone a new straightener," came Oma Mei's reply. To which she added, "And I can't really see what that has to do with the Virgin Mary, anyway."

"Don't you want to be the Virgin Mary?" I'd asked her when we were alone.

Jess was silent.

"It could be fun, couldn't it?" I'd urged. "Imagine—there are lots of angels, at least a hundred, but only three Virgin Marys."

"Just leave me alone," Jess had finally said.

It was recess. We left the classroom. On my way out, Muulke and I passed in the hallway. We signaled to each other because we weren't allowed to talk in the corridors. As soon as we got outside, Muulke started complaining about the chicken feathers for the angels' wings.

"I have to start all over again," she said. "Just because a couple of them aren't on exactly right. As if angels always have their wings perfectly tidy."

She looked at me imploringly.

"Don't even think about it," I said. "I already have enough to do."

"But it gives me a terrible headache," Muulke complained. "One of these days, I'm going to go blind." She peered at the statue of the Virgin Mary. "I'm sure my sight is already getting a lot worse," she said, giving me a hopeful look.

Ignoring her, I asked, "Where's Jess?"

"And then it will be all your fault."

"I don't see Jess."

"No point asking me," said Muulke furiously. "I can hardly see anything." But she looked around all the same. We both did, but couldn't see her anywhere.

"Maybe she's being kept in," said Muulke.

But that didn't make any sense, and she knew it as well as I. The only one who was forever being kept in was Muulke. I was too scared to ever do anything that was forbidden, and Jess was always spared because of her wreckbone. I suddenly felt uneasy. I remembered the girl from that morning who had told us to watch out.

Was it my imagination or were people looking at us out of the corners of their eyes? Were they whispering behind our backs?

"There is something strange going on," said Muulke. "Come on, we have to look for her."

"Where?" I asked.

"You look in the street," said Muulke. "And I'll look inside."

I was horrified. "Are you crazy?"

"What else do you want us to do?"

"You know perfectly well the only place we're allowed to be is the schoolyard. Not outside in the street and certainly not inside the building.

Muulke glared at me.

"Maybe she's still inside," I tried. "Maybe there's nothing wrong. Maybe it's a joke."

"And maybe if you wash coal for seven months it'll turn white," Muulke snarled. She turned around, and, without looking back, she walked to the school door, peered left, then right, and slipped back inside the building.

I heard Jess's voice before I was even outside the schoolyard.

"It's none of your business."

I walked past the outer brick wall. I already knew what I would see on the other side. I'd been secretly worried about this all along.

Jess was surrounded by Fat Tonnie's group. Although she was at least a head shorter than the rest, she looked more annoyed than scared.

Somehow, that gave me courage. "Leave my sister alone," I said calmly.

They turned on me.

"Aha, another one from outside the walls," said Fat Tonnie, in her slow, drawling voice. She smiled. She had yellowish, pointy teeth. "Keep your shirt on, Boon. We just wanted some information."

"Leave my sister alone," I said again.

"So you said," said Fat Tonnie.

"She must have swallowed a parrot," one of the other girls jeered.

The pack of them doubled over with laughter, but Fat Tonnie shut them up with one look.

"So she's the new Virgin Mary," said Fat Tonnie. She put her hands on Jess's shoulders. She had big hands and muscular arms. I now saw that Tonnie's nickname wasn't quite right; she wasn't so much fat as solid. They should have called her Tonnie the Bear.

"Well?" she asked.

"What is it to you?" asked Jess.

In one fluid movement, Fat Tonnie wrapped her arms around Jess. She did it with a smile. It could have been a game, if the faces of the other girls hadn't suddenly become so greedy and excited.

I felt all my calm ebb away.

"We're just curious," said one of them.

"Very curious," said Fat Tonnie, who kept a tight hold on Jess, even as she tried to wriggle out. But Jess was no match for Tonnie.

"What do you want?" I asked.

Fat Tonnie nodded at a girl who was standing at the back. "Do you think she's pretty?"

I stared at her, confused.

"Do you think she's pretty?" she repeated.

I nodded.

"Prettier than your sister?"

"Let her be," the pretty girl said suddenly. She spoke softly.

Fat Tonnie ignored her. "Prettier than your sister?"

I could feel myself growing hot and cold at the same time. I could feel Jess looking at me imploringly. But what could I do? The important thing was to gain time, and I wasn't going to succeed by giving the wrong answer.

When I answered, I didn't dare look at Jess.

"So she's prettier than your sister?" said Fat Tonnie.

"Yes."

"I can't hear you."

"Yes!"

I had expected Tonnie's group to burst out laughing, but instead they became dead still, which was a hundred times worse.

"And your sister is uglier."

"What do you want now?"

"Answer me."

I saw her arms tighten around Jess.

"Yes," I burst out. "She's uglier."

"She was supposed to be the Virgin Mary," said Fat Tonnie, tilting her head toward the pretty girl.

"I don't mind," the pretty girl said again. "Really."

Fat Tonnie looked at Jess, and her face became thoughtful.

"Newcomers never play the Virgin Mary. So why her? You said yourself she's ugly. And she's too small for a Virgin Mary. Mary's always a sixth-grader."

She laughed, baring her big yellow teeth. "Perhaps her beauty is all on the inside?"

I realized instantly what she was planning to do.

"Don't!" I yelled.

The group surrounded me, separating me from Jess. I wanted to resist, but my arms were as limp as a piece of string. Unlike Muulke, I wasn't a fighter. I was no threat, no savage soldier, no all-devouring monster. I wasn't even much good at playing a house.

Where was Muulke, for God's sake?

Then Jess started screaming.

Squeak-Creak

———

THERE WAS NO ONE in the kitchen, the living room, the bedrooms, or the attic, so Muulke and I walked around to the workshop. There, the door that used to be a window stood wide open, and the workshop was hazy with smoke.

Our brothers greeted us from behind tankards of beer as if we had been away for a year. We were surprised to see Oma Mei there, too. Hovering behind a large tankard, her face looked both surprised and bewildered. Her expression was so weird that if I hadn't been feeling so terrible, I would have laughed.

"How about a beer?" called Piet.

"Get something for those girls," called Eet.

"If a button-chewer runs off with your brandy," called Sjeer with a thick tongue, "you have to think of something else." He looked at us, his eyes bloodshot from smoke and alcohol.

"We had a miracle worker among us and we never knew it," said Krit.

At the workbench sat Oompah Hatsti, his unfocused eyes staring into the distance. He was turning out one cigar after another with amazing speed and precision.

"As straight and tight as the Juliana Canal," said Piet.

"What do you expect if you have your father's hands?" said Eet.

They watched the button-chewer's busy little hands.

"Why bother mechanizing if you have an Oompah Hatsi?" said Nol, who was there, too. His voice sounded almost jealous.

Had Oompah been making cigars at the institution? Or was it because he had mended clothes all his life, work that was just as precise? Or maybe the monotonous work calmed him down? Perhaps that was why he was concentrating so hard? We didn't know and we would never know, but the fact was that the button-chewer could single-handedly turn out cigars faster than Dad and our brothers combined. He rumbled and hummed like a well-oiled car engine.

"Is Jess here?" I asked.

Our grandmother looked up with a start. "Jess?"

"We thought she was here," said Muulke.

Her swivel-eye swung to the right. "What would she be doing here?"

"Umm…Jess got out of school earlier than we did."

"And why was that?"

"We…um…we had to stay behind," I said.

"Stay behind? Why?"

"A fight," Muulke said casually.

"Muulke Boon!" Oma Mei burst out. "How often have I told you not to fight!"

"They were pestering Jess," I said.

Muulke explained how Fat Tonnie and her group had taken Jess behind the outer wall and how they had tried to undo her clothes so they could see her straightener. I was more than happy for Muulke to do the talking; my legs were still shaking.

"*Kwatsj!*" said our grandmother, uncomprehendingly. "How would those girls know about her straightener, for God's sake?"

Muulke shrugged. "Perhaps they overheard you talking with the headmistress. Or they may have figured it out for themselves. They knew, anyway. And then we argued because they were angry that Jess was going to be the Virgin Mary, and then we had to see the headmistress."

"And then?"

"Then we had to stay behind," said Muulke. "Sister Angelica sent Jess home, to be on the safe side. Her straightener had gotten undone."

"She must have gone to see Fie," said Sjeer.

"Well, you lost her," said Oma Mei. "So you can go and find her."

Fie's mother opened the door. Muulke and I walked up the familiar steep stairs to the small landing. It was dark and stuffy. I had never noticed that before.

"Is Jess here?" we asked.

Fie's mother was peeling potatoes. Her hands were red.

"I don't know, *leeveke*. I've just come home. Maybe she's up in the attic with Fie."

The second staircase was even narrower and steeper. It was more like climbing a ladder than walking up a staircase. The attic really was just a large dormer window. There, behind wire netting, Fie's father kept his prize pigeons.

We saw Fie with a pigeon on her head. She wasn't surprised to see us, which was strange, or ought to have been strange, because during the last few months we had barely seen her. But just as Jess was Jess, and Muulke Muulke, so Fie was Fie. For a moment, I had a feeling of loss.

Fie laughed. "Hi."

"Hi," we said.

"Have you seen Jess?"

"Jess? No."

The pigeon pecked at the grains Fie kept putting on top of her head. She had to move very carefully.

Muulke made to leave, pulling me along with her.

"I'll drop in again soon," I said.

When we passed back through the tiny kitchen, I saw our old window across the street. It suddenly seemed like a very long time ago that we had lived there. As if it wasn't only a year that had passed, but a century. A colander stood on the windowsill. Somewhere a woman was singing, but nobody was to be seen.

It was no longer our house.

When we got home, the house was deserted apart from Oompah Hatsi. Meanwhile, the small stack had become quite a stack of straight, well-formed, firm cigars.

"Where is everybody?" we asked.

Oompah didn't look up.

We sat on the fence and waited.

"We should have listened to Jess more carefully," I said.

"All she had to do was talk to us," said Muulke.

"She did talk to us," I said. "She told us she wanted to go back to our old house."

"Jess says that every time we move."

"She said she hated the school."

"I say that all the time."

"Yes," I said. "But when you say it, it doesn't mean anything."

We were silent. It was a windy day. Sand blew up in gusts. Since we'd been living here, I couldn't run my hand through my hair without sand falling out. Some days the never-ending wind made me so tired! This was one of those days—a day when you wished you had no ears and no skin with which to feel everything.

"Nothing at all would have happened if Jess wasn't forever being told not to do this and not to do that," said Muulke.

"It's just that she's got that wreckbone," I said.

"Yes, so? She can't spend the rest of her life doing nothing, just because her back sometimes—"

"Last year she had to lie flat on her back for a whole month!"

"Most of the time she's all right."

"Because she's careful."

"Because she's not allowed to do anything. Nothing at all!"

"As long as she's careful, nothing happens."

"That time at school, all she wanted to do was tie her shoelace."

"You don't know what she'd done before that."

"You sound just like Oma Mei."

"But it's true, isn't it?"

"No," said Muulke. "It isn't true. You all think it's like that, but I think you're just making her worse. If everybody fussed about me like that, I'd get a wreckbone, too!"

I looked at her, bewildered.

"Jess just needs to be left in peace," she said.

"The way you leave everyone in peace, I suppose," I snarled. "The way it was your fault she got the wreckbone curse that time in the cemetery."

"You let her drag those tubs, not me."

"That's mean!" I shouted. "I didn't even know she'd loosened her straps."

"But tightening them was on your little list!" Muulke said triumphantly.

Angrily, I leaped off the fence. I walked down the road. My dress was flapping in the wind. I let myself be blown along. Behind the hedge, where Mr. Wetsels' field began, I stopped.

At times I felt like I could have murdered Muulke. It was mean of her to say it was our fault. Nobody could do anything about Jess's back. The doctors said that very few children have a loose vertebra. So how were we supposed to know all the right things to do if even the doctors themselves didn't know? Our grandmother might be very strict, but she only wanted to protect Jess, didn't she? The doctors said that sometimes a child could grow out of it, and that in adulthood the vertebra would just slip back into place on its own and stay there. Sometimes. In the meantime, the important thing was to make sure the bone didn't slip out of place. And that was why Jess wore the straightener. And that was why she slept in a special bed. And that was why she had to be careful about what she did. It wasn't true that she wasn't allowed to do anything. That was *kwatsj*!

A knocking sound interrupted my thoughts. I turned.

The little shed in the field looked more weather-beaten and dilapidated than ever. The door was blowing open and slamming shut.

That's when I heard another sound. It was between the opening and the closing of the door. Very soft, but unmistakable. A sound I could recognize anywhere.

"Jess?" I walked through the field. "Jess?"

We should have known. Here she was close enough to the house to feel safe, but far enough away to make a point. I stopped the door from shutting again and went in.

I couldn't see a thing, but there was no need.

"It's only me," I said, as relief flooded through my mind. I was already holding out my arms to hug her scared little body and hold her close.

I didn't need to see. All I had to do was listen. I had never been so happy to hear that sound.

Squeak-creak, squeak-creak.

Disappeared

THE KITCHEN WAS A hive of activity. Dad was trying to make coffee and was making a mess of it. Our brothers were dragging chairs around, knocking over anything in their way. Had Oma Mei been there, she'd have had a heart attack.

"She wasn't in any of our old houses," said our brothers.

"And not in her old school, either," said Dad.

"Where were you all this time?" asked Muulke.

I wanted to tell her, but somehow couldn't utter a single sound. So I showed her.

"What?" said Dad.

"How did you get hold of that?" asked Piet, Eet, Sjeer, and Krit.

"It was in the little shed in the field," I finally said. "Hanging on a nail. I heard it squeaking in the wind. I thought it was Jess."

They all stared at the straightener. Without Jess, it was even more of a monstrous thing—an instrument of torture from the Middle Ages. I looked at Muulke out of the corner of my eye, ready for her triumphant look. But she only looked worried. Then, when she saw me looking, she winked. I don't think I'll ever understand her.

We heard the gate opening and closing and quickly crowded outside.

It was Oma Mei.

She looked excited. For a moment, we thought she had found Jess.

"She's gone off to Maastricht," she called, panting.

Oma Mei had gone to see the doctor, and he had told her that Jess had come to see him a week ago. She had wanted to know if there were other straighteners for sale, and where you could buy them.

"Of course," I said. "She's been talking about that."

"Other straighteners?" Krit wondered.

"Ones that don't squeak-creak," said Oma Mei.

"*Miljaar! Miljaar!*" cried Sjeer.

"All that way!" said Krit.

"And without a straightener!" Eet exclaimed.

"It'll be dark soon, too," Dad muttered.

As usual, our grandmother was the first to come to her senses.

"Piet, Krit, and Antoon, you'll take the bus to Maastricht. Jess may be walking along the main road. If that's the case, you should be able to spot her soon enough. Otherwise, wait at the bus station in Maastricht. Eet, Sjeer, and I will take the back roads."

"I'd like to walk, too," said Dad.

"I know the way better."

"Won't it be too tiring for you?"

She glared at him. "I can still walk the socks off you,

Antoon Boon. Every day, if I have to."

"And us?" asked Muulke and I.

"You stay here," said Oma Mei.

"But…"

"You stay here. In case she changes her mind, or we miss her."

They made sandwiches, took a bottle of water each, and set off. The last thing we saw was our grandmother walking, or rather trotting, past Eet and Sjeer, in the reddish light of the late afternoon sun.

"No running, and stay together," said Muulke, but I couldn't manage a laugh.

In a Tangle of Arms and Legs

THE WORST THING THAT night was the waiting. We had no idea how long everyone would be away. I sighed and sighed, until Muulke finally glared at me angrily.

"Stop it," she snarled. "That *sjiethoes* will be back all right."

But a single look at her pale face was enough to tell me she wasn't so sure herself. Poor Muulke. All her life she had invented so many stories full of calamity, murder, and bloodshed that now she couldn't stop imagining the worst.

"Tell me it'll be all right," she said miserably. "Tell me it'll be all right, or I'll…or I'll…"

For the first time ever, her imagination failed her.

"It will be all right," I said.

I tidied up the workshop and washed the dishes. I brought *sjlamm* up from the cellar. I peeled potatoes and scraped the beetroots. We cooked and ate without talking.

How often I had wished I could be by myself, without the constant slamming of doors, the creaking of staircases, the sound of squabbling coming through the walls and cracks… but now those sounds seemed like the loveliest in the whole world.

"They're here," Muulke said every five minutes. Then she'd race outside and I'd feel panic rising up inside me and shout that she shouldn't leave me alone.

Night fell. We'd forgotten what an isolated house Nine Open Arms was. A restless house, too: it groaned and moaned, creaked and rattled. All I could think of was Jess. Jess all by herself in the dark, Jess in her thin summer dress without a straightener.

"It's as if we're alone in the world," Muulke said dully. "As if we're not half-orphans but real orphans."

"Stop it now," I said.

"Terrible things happen on the road to Maastricht," said Muulke. "Last year a tree blew over and struck a woman. And someone was murdered there once, a man, still a boy, really, and the murderer was never—"

"Shut up your stupid face!" I screamed.

Muulke was scared. I was scared, too. I had never screamed like that in my life. It was as if my mouth was no longer my own.

"You have to stop, Muulke," I said, shaking. "You're terrifying both of us."

And then the waiting started again. Or did it just continue? I didn't know. All I knew was that time passed horribly slowly.

At some point, we must have fallen asleep on the sofa with a blanket over us. We hadn't wanted to go up to our bedroom. That would have felt like a betrayal. All I remember is that one moment it was pitch-dark, the middle of the night. The next, I saw the sun shining over the hedge. The window stood ajar with a rag in the gap to stop it from rattling. We had opened it so we wouldn't fall asleep. It was cool in the house.

I woke up with a clear head. For the first time in two weeks I hadn't had a nightmare. Muulke was still asleep. She was half-hanging off the sofa, with her head at a strange angle.

"Muulke."

She opened her eyes. We lay together in silence for a while. We didn't move. Neither of us wanted to feel how we were lying there with our four pathetic arms and legs.

"The stupid, dumb *sjiethoes*," said Muulke.

"Yes, I miss her, too," I said.

A blackbird landed on top of the hedge and started singing. As if that was the sign for time to start moving again, Oompah walked past. He stumbled down the garden path toward the hedge. I heard him grumbling and muttering. He had outdone himself this time; in his arms he carried a stack of plates, some cups, a sheet, and the cutlery box. On top of it all, the glass jug from our kitchen wobbled precariously.

"That's just what we need," Muulke muttered.

I got up shivering and put my shoes on.

"Will you make coffee?" I asked before going out, adding as casually as I could manage, "They could be here at any moment."

That was enough to get Muulke moving.

As I walked past the fence, I saw Oompah disappearing into the hedge.

The grass was still damp, the sky bright blue. The twigs of the hedge tickled my bare arms. The smell of fire was still noticeable.

Once I was through the hedge, something stopped me

from walking toward Oompah. The button-chewer stood silently by the nameless grave, and some of his treasures were displayed on the grass. The glass jug glittered in the sun. Behind him, on top of the gravestone, lay the burlap sack, bulging with more treasures. He stood very still, as if he had never moved and would never move again.

The sun's rays came over the top of the hedge. I had to squint against the fierce light. Oompah became a silhouette, like in the photos from the Crocodile.

I don't know how long I stood there, how long it took. I just know I became deeply aware of something—of how ridiculous it was that I had wasted all my time thinking and worrying about that nameless grave. If I hadn't been so preoccupied with myself, I would have noticed how very unhappy Jess was. And she wouldn't have run away.

"Saint Rosa," I said softly. "Will you please look after her? And make sure she comes home safely? Then I promise I will never get worked up again about that stupid gravestone."

It was as if a big load had fallen from my shoulders. As if I'd become the old Fing again. The blackbird, which had been silent, started to sing again, as if it was trying to bring summer back all by itself. The trees around us started rustling again, too.

I took a deep breath. The scents of earth, grass, and summer penetrated my nostrils.

Then the photo started to move and the spell was broken. But it was a full second before I realized that it wasn't Oompah who had moved.

I gasped.

It was the burlap sack.

No *Sjiethoes*

———

SHE WAS STILL WARM with sleep. She blinked against the sunlight, laughed, and said, "I wasn't scared at all."

I wanted to hit her. I wanted to hug her. I wanted to cry and to laugh, but all I did was clear my throat and kneel down next to her. Only her head and a tangle of rags stuck out of the sack. She had stayed warm.

Jess was back. My Jess was back.

"Why aren't you in Maastricht?" I said as sternly as I could.

She stared at me, confused. There was a sleep crease in her cheek.

"Maastricht?" she giggled.

"Wasn't that where you were going?"

She looked at me sleepily. "Maastricht?"

I told her what Oma Mei had heard from the doctor.

She tapped her forehead. "I just wanted to know. I'd hardly walk all the way to Maastricht on my own. In the middle of the night? I'm not completely crazy."

She hadn't gone to Maastricht. She hadn't been walking along the side of the road in the dark. I couldn't help it; I burst out laughing. And then I nearly cried, I was so relieved.

"You'll catch a cold if you're not careful," I said. It had nothing to do with anything, I knew. "Weren't you scared?"

"I was at first," said Jess with a yawn. "But Oompah gave me the sack to crawl into and rags to keep me warm. He kept watch."

She sat up, and without realizing it, I raised my arm and put it around her. How well she fit! How well she fit into the crook of my arm. How could anything be so right?

The button-chewer grumbled. When I looked up, he lowered his eyes, took out his scissors, and vigorously started snipping the air to shreds. But he would never be able to fool me again.

How crazy could he be if for a whole night he kept watch so that nothing would happen to a scared little girl? If he brought her rags for warmth (as if he knew about the rag-doll heart), and a sack to crawl into? And how confused could he be if he knew just how to lure her sister to the cemetery the following morning?

We sat for a while.

"Is she angry?" Jess asked.

"Mostly, she's really frightened."

"Oma Mei is forever really frightened." Jess yawned again.

"Maybe she is." I kissed the top of her head. "Why didn't you come straight home?"

"To begin with I was angry at Muulke, and at you. Then, once I had stayed away for a couple of hours, I was scared of Oma Mei and what she would say." Jess was silent for a moment. "I came here because I knew you wouldn't look for me here."

That was true. It was the last place we would have looked for her.

"When it got dark, I really wanted to come home. But after a while, I wanted to stay here." She looked me in the eyes. "Why am I always so scared, Fing?"

"I don't think you're scared," I said.

"I'm always the *sjiethoes*," said Jess.

"You're not half as much of a *sjiethoes* as I am," I said. "Anyway, a real *sjiethoes* doesn't sleep all night in a cemetery."

We were silent again for a while.

"Let's go home," I said. "I want to see Muulke's face. She thinks you've been murdered a hundred times over."

Jess grinned.

"A tragical tragedy," we said in unison and laughed.

"Shall I dress up as a ghost?" Jess's eyes shone and for a moment she looked just like Muulke.

"Don't you dare," I said. "You've given us enough of a fright already."

We got up.

"Oompah? Are you coming?"

The button-chewer pretended not to hear, so I left it at that.

"Jess."

"Yes?"

"You mustn't ever run away again, do you hear? Never, ever again."

She nodded. We went through the opening in the hedge.

"What's Muulke doing?"

"Making coffee."

"Muulke?"

We grinned and crossed the road. Through the open window, we heard our sister pottering about, accompanied by many a "*Miljaar!*"

"*Miljaar!*" I muttered, too, for I'd forgotten all about the stuff Oompah had taken. "Wait a minute. I'll be right back." I turned around, retracing our steps.

The Wanderer of
Sjlammbams Sahara

I'VE OFTEN WONDERED WHETHER we ever would have worked
it out if Jess hadn't run away and hidden in the cemetery
because she knew we wouldn't come looking for her there.

Now, so many years later, I'm still not certain of the answer.

Is it true that some stories only just manage to be born? Or
do these stories always seek their own path into the world and
do they always, eventually, find a way of being told?

As I walked back into the cemetery, I saw something. I saw
Oompah Hatsi sitting down.

That was all.

He sat down on the gravestone without a name and crossed
his arms, like he was waiting.

It may have been the way he looked or how he sat, I don't
know, but it was as if I had been blind and suddenly could see.
I looked at Oompah Hatsi, the ageing button-chewer, sitting
on the stone slab, but that is not what I saw. What I saw was a
boy, a child. The child from my dreams: the young Oompah
Hatsi, waiting for Nienevee to come out. The young Oompah

Hatsi who had to wait for his mother and sat himself down on the…

I gasped.

"What's the matter?" said Jess when I came out through the hedge again.

I didn't reply but walked straight past her and across Sjlammbams Sahara, racing through the gate, around the corner, and right to the front door at the back of the house. I stopped, panting, and Dad's words flashed through my mind: *A front door at the back, a threshold at knee height, is this a house full of surprises or what?*

I stared at the threshold, which was so high we had to literally clamber into the house. I could have kicked myself. "That grave isn't Charley's grave at all!" I shouted.

"Which grave?" cried Jess, who'd run after me.

"The grave with no name. That isn't his grave at all."

Jess frowned.

"That's why there is no name and no date on it!" I shouted. "And why there is only a flat slab!"

"So whose grave is it?" Jess asked cautiously.

I began to laugh. "It isn't a grave at all!"

"Then what is it?"

I laughed even more. "It's the doorstep!"

"The what?"

"The doorstep of Nine Open Arms!"

Jess stared at me as if I'd gone mad.

"It's the doorstep Nienevee always wanted when she was still a child and that she got when she married Van Wessum!"

It had occurred to me the moment Oompah sat down. I had seen the little boy who sat on the doorstep of Townies'

Welcome, waiting for his mother to come out.

"But who moved that doorstep all the way to the cemetery?" asked Jess. "And why?"

I stared at the door, frowning. I kept looking at the four holes above it. My feeling of disquiet became stronger.

Something began to glimmer in my mind. I didn't know yet what it was, but it was getting closer.

"What did Nienevee always say?" I asked.

"What do you mean?"

"'I spit on the travelers. I spit on the...' How did it go again?"

"Townspeople. Only the other way round. But why do you want to know?"

There was something there. There was something about those words.

"Please say it," I said. "Please say it exactly as she said."

Jess thought for a moment. "I spit on the townspeople," she repeated obediently. "I spit on the travelers. I spit on the whole world if it comes right down to it. And I'll show them, too." She looked at me doubtfully.

Finally, I'd got it. Finally, I knew what wasn't right.

I took a deep breath. "If you really want to show that you spit on the whole world, why hide your front door at the back? It just isn't logical. Particularly if you've had a sign specially made saying 'Townies' Welcome' and you want everyone to see it. It just doesn't make sense."

"Nor does putting the doorstep of your house in the cemetery," said Jess. "Who would do a thing like that?"

I hope you can find rest now.

I heard Oma Mei's voice so loud and clear that I thought for a moment she was standing right next to me. But she wasn't.

It was only her voice in my head.

I hope you can find rest now.

These were the words that made everything fall into place.

Flabbergasted, I stared from the house to the cemetery, from the holes above the front door to the high threshold, and then to the hedge, behind which lay the doorstep of Nine Open Arms.

Now that I understood, it was strange to think that we hadn't seen it before. There had been so many signs.

A letter that couldn't find our house.

A front door at the back.

And, above all, the image of our grandmother standing by the staircase while Jess was being carried upstairs. Oma Mei leaning forward as if she was facing a storm.

I hope you can find rest now.

First, we'd thought it was Nienevee who had to find rest. Later, Oma Mei had said she meant Oompah. But that wasn't it, either. The answer had been closer to home. Much closer. So close, in fact, that we'd completely overlooked it. It was our house. It had been Nine Open Arms all along.

"We've been thinking the wrong way around," I said simply. "It's not the doorstep that's been moved."

At the end of Sjlammbams Sahara stood a house.

The house of Nine Open Arms.

Once, it had had a different name.

Once, there were different people living in it.

And once, it had stood somewhere else.

Fight

___

OMA MEI PUT JESS to bed. We heard her moving around upstairs.

Muulke and I waited resignedly downstairs.

"Now we're in for it," said Muulke, when Oma Mei came down.

I sat at the table trying to put some order into my thoughts. Oma Mei stood there, arms akimbo, her face pale and stern.

"From Muulke I could understand it," she said. "That one has never had an ounce of responsibility in her. But from you, I can't believe it. You should have stayed with Jess."

I could feel my cheeks burning. "I was being kept in, too," I said.

"You should have told them right away that you had nothing to do with it."

"But…" I said.

"If Muulke starts lashing out in all directions, she'll have to suffer the consequences. You should have known better. Muulke can look after herself. I don't dare think about what could have happened to Jess."

My heart shrank.

"Without her straightener. Dear God!"

"Fortunately, it's all turned out all right in the end," Dad said soothingly.

But Oma Mei had no intention of letting herself be soothed. "What if she had started walking?" she spluttered. "What if something had happened?"

"But nothing did happen," said Muulke. "Jess just stayed here. And if you ask me, it's all her fault. No one told her to run off and hide and stay away the whole night."

Oma Mei turned to Muulke. "I don't think I asked for your opinion. I may have resigned myself to the fact that you're never going to be a real lady, but that doesn't mean I have to put up with your insolence. And it certainly doesn't mean you can go around pulling bunches of hair out of people's heads like some cheap street girl."

Muulke looked at her with burning cheeks, but didn't say anything.

"She's practically bald on one side!" Oma Mei shouted furiously.

I can't say how it happened, but as I watched the scene, I suddenly found my courage. "That wasn't Muulke," I said.

"Leave it," said Muulke.

"What's that?" shouted Oma Mei.

"Just leave it," Muulke said again.

Oma Mei stared at me.

"I did it," I said.

"Don't be ridiculous," said Oma Mei. "Who's going to believe that you..."

Her voice wavered. She looked at me and I could see that it was only now that she was really seeing me. I still had yesterday's clothes on and one of the sleeves of my dress was torn. My elbows were cut and my hair ribbon was in tatters.

Oma Mei gasped for breath. "You…?"

I nodded.

My brothers whistled. Whether in admiration or fright, I couldn't say. Dad laughed, and that was probably the last straw.

"What sort of a family is this!" Oma Mei exploded. "Have you all gone crazy? Jess throws out her straightener. Muulke secretly steals jars of preserves and nearly does in Oompah Hatsi. And now you go and get into a fight?"

I bit my lip.

"What should she have done?" demanded Muulke. "Do you think she should have stood by and watched them making a fool of Jess? Right until they'd displayed her wreckbone to the whole school?"

"You should have called one of the nuns."

"They weren't around," said Muulke. "And by the time I found out where Jess and Fing were, the fight had already begun. And if you want to know my opinion, I think what Fing did is fantastic. It was that stupid girl's own stupid fault. She should have kept her paws off Jess." Her eyes sparkled.

"I don't think I asked for your opinion," said Oma Mei. "But now that you've given it anyway, I'll tell you what I think about all of you. I am so glad your mother didn't have to live through all of this. With her rag-doll heart, she wouldn't have survived."

Maybe it was those words that made me do it. Maybe it was Oma's reproaches.

"You have lied to us," I said.

Silence fell. A deeper silence than there had ever been in

Nine Open Arms.

"I beg your pardon?" spluttered Oma Mei.

"You've lied to us," I repeated. "And that's much worse."

I heard my brothers and Dad breathe in, all at exactly the same moment.

"Listen," said Dad. "Perhaps we should—"

"Wait!" Oma Mei interrupted him. "I would like to know what my oldest granddaughter has to say." She glared at me with her good eye, now icy cold. Her look made me wish my words could crawl back into my mouth, but I forced myself to go on.

"You said you had burned the tombstone bed, but it's sitting in Mr. Wetsels' little shed. And you said that it was Oompah who had to find rest. But that wasn't true, either."

I was vaguely aware there was some confusion in the room. Dad stared at Oma Mei. Our brothers were frowning. And Oma Mei was all flushed, but not just with an ordinary blush. Rather, fiery red splotches had broken out on her face and neck.

"What are you saying to me?" Her voice was soft, but dangerous. I had known her my whole life, so I knew exactly when she was at her most dangerous. Up until now that had always been the moment I shut up. But I couldn't do that anymore. I felt a fury rising in me that was so huge and strange that it was as if I was transforming into a different person.

"Why haven't you told us that the house used to stand in the cemetery?" I shouted.

Her swivel-eye made a wild sweep.

"What?" Dad was confused.

"What?" shouted Piet, Eet, Krit, and Sjeer.

"What on earth does that have to do with anything?" shouted Oma Mei.

So it was true. She was admitting it. It was true!

"That makes three times you've lied already."

"Fing, stop it right now," said Dad. "And Oma Mei, please, you have to calm down."

But we were facing each other and nothing could stop us now.

"How dare you speak to me like that?" Oma shouted. "To me, your own grandmother." She lashed out at me, but Piet jumped between us and caught the blow.

I dove behind the kitchen table.

"You lie!" I screamed.

"How dare you!" shouted my grandmother. She tried to come after me, but Dad and Eet stopped her.

"Calm down now! Calm down, let us—"

"You are always lying!" The words flew out of my mouth, coming on their own, as if they had nothing to do with me. All I had to do was open my mouth. It was terrible and wonderful at the same time.

"You are a liar!"

"Watch out, *kendj*. I am still your—"

"And who knows what else you've been lying about? You, with your Crocodile stories. How true are those stories, really? What sort of lies have you been telling us about our mother? Or about Opa Pei?" My voice cracked.

Oma Mei flinched. I had never seen her flinch, never seen her take a step back. Nobody had ever seen that. I heard Dad gasp.

There was another silence, an even more terrible silence. It was as if sound itself was disappearing through an invisible hole in the house.

"I don't think I like being called a liar by my own granddaughter." Oma Mei was trying to say this in an icy tone, but I could feel that something in her authority had broken down. Her voice wavered, as did the harshness on her face.

"Listen," Dad said soothingly. "We're all dead tired. There will be plenty of time for being angry, so why don't you go and have a good sleep, Fing. And tomorrow we'll—"

My fury burst out all over again. "And why the heck are we forever leaving places? Why can't we ever stay somewhere? Why don't we ever visit Mother's grave anymore? It's not true that she is everywhere. That's another lie, a dirty filthy lie. Just like the opposite of worrying, just like first believing, then seeing. You two are always lying till you're blue in the face."

Lowering my voice, I turned to Oma Mei. "And why are we only allowed to ask the questions you want us to ask? Why can't we ever ask questions of our own?"

"Be quiet," Oma Mei said shaking.

"Why do we always have to wait until you're ready to tell us something? That is just so mean."

"Be quiet!"

"And there are other things I want to know," I sobbed. "I want to know how our mother died. Why she went with Dad to live somewhere else instead of staying in the same town with you. Why she was buried there and not here. And I damn well want to know what it was she died of."

With every question our grandmother took a step back, until she had retreated out of the kitchen. She stumbled away. I heard her climbing the stairs, rummaging around upstairs, and coming down again. She stood in the passage, holding the broken Crocodile in her arms, her face gray.

Now we were both crying.

"I may not do everything right," she sobbed. "I may not be the best grandmother ever. But if that's how it is, you should say it. Nobody ever says anything around here."

"Go away!" I shouted in tears.

Before we realized what was happening and before anyone could do anything about it, our grandmother walked down the passage, wrenched open the front doot, and walked out of the house with the Crocodile in her arms.

Without looking or remembering, she stepped through the door with its knee-high threshold—the only front door in the town that stood nearly fifty feet away from its doorstep.

Windblown Memories

THE PHOTOS WERE EVERYWHERE. They stirred in the grass and in the vegetable garden. They got stuck behind the cellar windows. They fluttered across Sjlammbams Sahara and into the hedge.

"There's one," called Oma Mei from the kitchen window. "And there."

We ran around Nine Open Arms collecting them one by one.

She was sitting on the sofa, her bandaged-up left foot resting on a chair. I brought in the photos I'd picked up. She took them without looking at me. I was no longer angry, or rather I was still angry, but I no longer felt guilty about it.

"That wasn't nice of you, *kendj*," said Oma Mei. "And with me already standing with one-and-a-half feet in my grave." I chanted along with her. She pressed her lips into a thin line, and I thought she was about to say something nasty, but her mouth relaxed, and she let out a sigh.

We were silent for a while.

"How's your foot?" I asked.

"Not too bad."

"Shall I bring you another cushion?"

"Just let me be for a little."

We were silent again for some time. I heard Muulke call out, "In the tree, in the tree." And our brothers shouted out all sorts of ideas about how to get the photos out of the tree.

"I hope we'll find all of them," I said.

"They're only photos," said Oma Mei. I could hear she didn't really believe that, but it was incredibly brave of her to say it. I wanted to throw my arms around her, but I couldn't. Not yet.

Oma Mei made a sound somewhere between a laugh and a cry. I looked up. She had the photos I had found in her hands and was looking at them.

I hadn't noticed which ones I'd picked up as I was collecting them. Still, I wasn't surprised when I saw which photo was on top. It was the one of Opa Pei. The photo of him and his workmen. Opa Pei in his stylish clothes and his felt hat.

I knew by the way she was looking at that photo which one it was.

"The story of Nienevee and Charley isn't finished yet, is it?" I said.

She shook her head.

Tell Me Why

MANY STORIES CAN BE told about a person's life. And each of our stories is connected by thin threads to those of many others. But the stories of Nienevee from Outside the Walls and Charley Bottletop weren't tied together until the end of their lives.

Thirty-two years had passed. It was 1902, and there was Charley, standing on her doorstep.

Much had happened. The nineteenth century had become the twentieth. A railway line had come to the town. New neighborhoods had grown up and new roads had been laid out. Much had changed, but not everything.

"So, Bottletop, here you are at last," said Nienevee, fifty years old and one week a widow.

He had arrived in town the evening before and had spent the night in a simple guesthouse. He had packed his bag at first light. It was drizzling a little when he walked through the unguarded Putse Gate. There was no reason to have guards at the gate now that most people lived outside the town walls.

And yet, he still had that same feeling as when he had left the town in his youth. It made him feel scared and happy at the same time.

Sjlammbams Sahara looked gray and deserted. November wasn't a month for farmers or for travelers, and certainly not for lovers, since all the tall corn was already gone. But for a dog named Dimdog, it was a good month. Dimdog was everywhere. She waited for Charley among the stubble of the cornfield. She wagged her tail by the oak trees at the dip in the slope. Putting down his bag, Charley threw a stick, and Dimdog ran after it. Dogs will be dogs, even if they've been dead for thirty years.

"So, Bottletop," said Nienevee.

There was so much he wanted to tell her, so much that had to be put right. There were reproaches and declarations of love thirty years old. Questions that had gone unanswered for so long that they had gone their own way, each looking for its own answer. How angry he had been at first, and how sad, and these feelings had been followed by years of indifference, he thought, and then…

She kissed him.

Nienevee, ex-traveler and brand-new widow, kissed Charley Bottletop right on the mouth. And when she had finished, she said, "Now all the old words are gone. Now all the pain is gone."

"Good," he said.

Not that it was true. The pain was still there, of course, but when you've just fallen in love all over again, you'll lie to yourself to infinity and back again. And you'll say yes and amen to anything, even if you are almost an old man.

The biggest surprise was waiting for him in the bedroom.

"Why?" he asked, astonished.

"Why not?" was her reply.

There stood the tombstone bed, smaller and grayer than he remembered it. Suddenly, he felt ashamed.

"You weren't to blame," she said.

He heard the sadness in her words, along with the anger and the bitterness, but there was no resignation.

She never told him about their son, the orphan who wasn't an orphan, who, on his sixteenth birthday, left town without a word. What could she have said? Sometimes words only make things worse. Sometimes it is better to be silent.

Love that becomes calmer over the years was not something Nienevee understood. After a one-day-and-one-night honeymoon, words flew every day, and plates, too, at times. Even though Charley couldn't understand her fits of rage or her deep sorrow, he let her rant and rave, because it meant her heart was still beating, and that somehow he could try to make up for all her pain, even if he hadn't caused it all. She was Nienevee, had always been, and would always stay that way. Her house, and all of the expensive things in it, couldn't change that.

"My Nienevee," he said.

Every night they slept in the tombstone bed, and then Nienevee would become the old Nienevee again. She would wrap her arms around him, and they would talk—about Lexidently and the night he and she fell on top of Charley; about the house Charley had made in the cornfield; about how Nienevee had known then that she loved him.

After, she would fall asleep, and he would twist and turn,

like a chair leg in a lathe. He swore he never slept a wink in the tombstone bed.

"It's as if we're buried already," he said.

"Better start getting used to it," she said.

He sketched out a design for a new bed. But she laughed in his face at the little kissing angels and the nesting birds passing each other twigs.

"Sentimental *kwatsj*," she said.

And when Charley wasn't looking, she set fire to the sketches. To keep the whole house from going up in flames, Charley decided to forget all about it.

They had nothing to do with the town, and the town had nothing to do with them. The scandal of the traveler widow living with a man she wasn't married to was only whispered about by the older people. The more recent townspeople barely knew who Charley and Nienevee were.

One day a letter arrived. Nienevee read it and turned pale. Charley asked what the matter was, but she didn't take the time to answer him. Instead, she slipped on her overcoat and marched off to the town hall, outraged. "Don't think for a moment you can pull this over on me," she shouted and spat across the counter.

"But, madam," said the startled clerk. "This was decided by the city council, not me."

"I spit on the city council," said Nienevee. "I spit on the whole world if it comes right down to it."

The town had grown considerably in the past half century, and where more people live, more people die. The old cemetery was now surrounded by new housing, and a new cemetery was needed in a spot outside the town where it could expand. And this meant somewhere along Sjlammbams Sahara.

Charley couldn't understand what she was making such a fuss about. The Council said they would provide a replacement house, at least as spacious as the one she was living in.

"That's a good thing, isn't it?" said Charley.

But she said—no, she screamed—that no one would ever get her out of her house.

"But you don't even really like it," Charley said.

But she screamed—no, she howled—that she'd been told too many times already that travelers should know their place. She swore she wouldn't take it this time, no, not this time, he could be sure of that.

So Charley left it at that. He wasn't going to argue. If Nienevee wanted to stay, he would stay, too.

Then fate struck. One day, Charley cut himself on a gouge, his hand became swollen, and two days later he was dead.

Blood poisoning.

Sometimes dying can be as simple as living is complicated.

Nienevee went looking for a gravestone for her Bottletop.

"That one?" The stonemason sounded surprised.

Nienevee nodded.

"A family gravestone?" said the stonemason.

"That's right," said Nienevee. And she told him—no, commanded him—what words to carve on the stone. That evening, the oldies in the cafe had another story to shout at each other about that traveler woman.

"She wants to be buried with Charley!"

The ancient parish priest got involved. "Only those whom God has joined in Holy Matrimony shall lie in one grave."

She chased him out of the door with a frying pan.

That was Nienevee from Outside the Walls. She wasn't careful or clever in how she went about things.

Meetings were held. Important meetings, involving even the Mayor. A new proposal was drawn up. An official came to tell her. He took care to stay close to the door; he had heard the story of the parish priest and the frying pan.

"You will be buried together and you will not have to go and live in another house, but the house must be moved," said the official.

Stunned, Nienevee stared at him. "Moved?"

"We have people who know how to do that," said the official. And he showed her on the survey map where the house would go.

Nienevee signed the expropriation document.

Two days later, surveyors started drawing lines and putting down markers. Nienevee saw them from her window.

"A high price to pay to be buried with you?" she said, as if dead Charley, who was laid out in the living room, had asked her something. "Not at all, Bottletop."

But nobody could tell if it was only Charley she was crying for when he, the first occupant of the new cemetery, was buried. So new was the cemetery that the priest had to bless Charley's plot. Trees had to be pruned and fields trimmed into lawns. Eventually, there would be a tall hedge. But Nienevee and Charley's grave was there first.

A week later, they started pulling down the house. First, they removed the roof tiles, then the roof beams. The timber frame was dismantled, too, so all that was left between the two chimneys was a gaping hole. The floors were pulled up board by board.

And so, brick by brick and plank by plank, the house was demolished. Then, brick by brick and plank by plank, it was rebuilt.

After that, Nienevee never found her feet again. She became restless and started wandering. She would accost complete strangers and tell them about herself and Charley.

Barely a year later, she died. She was found on the sofa, because after Charley's death she never slept in the tombstone bed again. In death, her face bore a mistrustful expression, and that mistrust was not for nothing.

It was never clear who had a hand in it, but one January day, Nienevee was carried away from her house. Away from Sjlammbams Sahara. Away from the new cemetery where the man she loved was buried. Away to the town she had hated. To the wrong grave with the wrong man.

Two Drops of Water

OUTSIDE, EVERYBODY WAS STILL busily finding photos. I heard
Muulke call out. Dad tapped on the window to find out, first
from Oma Mei and then from me, if everything was all right.
He disappeared again without waiting for an answer.

For a while, neither of us spoke.

"They were like two drops of water," Oma Mei said then.

"Who?"

"Your grandfather and your father." She laughed, but it
didn't sound cheerful. "They never knew each other. Opa Pei
died a year before your mother met your father, but if they had
known each other, I'm sure they would have become friends.
They shouldn't have been father- and son-in-law, but father
and son."

I waited patiently. I had no idea what Nienevee's story had
to do with my father and grandfather, but I also knew that Oma
Mei was going to tell me. She was going to tell me everything.
All I had to do was sit there until she stopped speaking.

"Both of them—dreamers of the worst kind," said
Oma Mei.

I stared at her. "Opa Pei as well as dad?"

"Your grandfather was the biggest dreamer of all. If they'd held a contest, he would have won easily. A hundred and twelve trades, a thousand and thirteen disasters: that was Opa Pei.

She stared at the photo, and I looked with her. I saw her good eye glide over my grandfather, over his silk vest and felt hat.

"But Opa Pei was a supervisor all his life, wasn't he?" I was confused.

Oma Mei didn't look at me.

She took out her handkerchief, blew her nose, pulled herself together, and started to speak again. This time, it wasn't a grand, dramatic history of a traveler woman and her impossible love that she had to tell, but a small story about Opa Pei, the dreamer, and the woman who thought she would be able to control him. About jobs and occupations that never lasted for more than a few months. About money that always ran out too soon. About promises and more promises. And about the demand that Oma Mei made on him when she finally became pregnant with the child she hadn't dared to hope for anymore—the demand to get a steady job or get lost.

"He was apprenticed to a cousin," said Oma Mei, "who was a prominent builder. So Opa Pei became a student; a student-supervisor at the age of forty-two. I was pleased he had steady work, even though it didn't pay much. But I was ashamed, too. He, on the other hand, always laughed about it. That's when this photo was taken. He had swapped clothes with his cousin, to tease me."

I took another look at the photo. So that's why the man

standing behind Opa Pei was laughing so hard. He wasn't a workman at all, but the builder himself.

Another silence followed. Oma Mei shifted her foot with a groan. Then she heaved a deep, deep sigh. I smiled at her, but I don't think she noticed.

"It happened a year after that photo was taken. Opa Pei's cousin got the job of moving Nienevee's house. But just the week before he had accepted another order, an important order, and he had sent his supervisor to oversee that job. So he left Nienevee's house to Opa Pei. And of course things went wrong. Horribly wrong."

She took out her handkerchief and blew her nose again. While I waited for her to continue, I looked out the window and saw Muulke crossing Sjlammbams Sahara with a broom. Piet teetered on Eet's shoulders, trying to get hold of a photo that was stuck on the top of the hedge. Sparrows flew up from the branches and disappeared into the corn.

Oma Mei cleared her throat.

"What happened then, Oma?"

She laughed scornfully. "Better ask what didn't happen. First, he forgot to prop up the house when they were taking it down. So when they were chiseling the bricks, one of the chimneys came loose. It collapsed and came within a hairsbreadth of crushing one of the men. Fortunately, it fell on the doorstep instead."

"So that's why there's that crack in the stone," I said.

"And that is why the doorstep stayed behind in the cemetery," said Oma Mei. "It couldn't be used any more. They were meant to provide a new one and to remove the old one, but that never happened. So many things never happened."

I mulled it all over. More and more things were falling into place; more and more riddles were being solved. The pieces of the puzzle were now fitting together. Except for one thing.

"I still can't understand why the front door of Nine Open Arms is at the back."

"That was the last, and probably the worst, mistake your grandfather made," said Oma Mei. "When he moved the house, he simply moved it along in a straight line, as if it was a cardboard box that was in the way. It just never occurred to him to turn the house around so it would face the road again. And when your grandfather's cousin came to have a look, the house was so far advanced that they decided to leave it as it was."

"And so the front door became the back door," I said.

She was silent.

The clock in the living room struck the hour. Outside, the hunt for photos was just about over. I heard Krit and Sjeer talking about money and all the things that lay ahead.

I took Oma's hand. Her calloused hand had unexpected soft spots. I had always known that, but for some reason I always forgot.

"Oma."

"Yes, *kendj*?"

I thought. There was something I wanted to say, but I didn't quite know what it was. Then, as I looked at her, the words started coming all by themselves.

"I don't really mind."

"What, *kendj*?"

"That Opa Pei wasn't a real supervisor."

She looked at me silently.

"Maybe it isn't such a good house," I said. "But it's his house. Sort of, anyway. And that makes it our house."

"Our ruin, you mean," Oma Mei said scornfully.

But she kept looking at me, and I looked back at her. And I kept on looking at her, and her swivel-eye didn't move once.

Muulke stormed into the room. "We've got them all. Or almost. There's one stuck behind the drainpipe. But if I climb out of the attic window—"

"Don't even think of it," Oma Mei interrupted. "Boys aren't girls and girls aren't..."

"Boys," the three of us sang together.

Muulke looked from me to Oma Mei, grinning.

"Are you still fighting?"

That's what Muulke was like. She'd ask anything, say anything, always speak her mind. I never knew whether to be horribly jealous or greatly relieved that I wasn't more like her.

She plopped herself down next to Oma Mei

"So was I right? Was there a tragedy or wasn't there?"

"A tragical tragedy," I said. I wanted to say it as a joke, but it didn't come out that way.

It wasn't a laughing matter to discover that tragical tragedies really exist in life, or to learn that sometimes they happen closer to home than you ever would have guessed.

One Foot

___

IN THE PROCESSION ON Saint Rosa's Day, I was the neatest girl, Muulke was the sloppiest, and Jess the most radiant.

Poised and solemn, all of us schoolgirls walked along in step in a long single line. Before the holiday, with a devout frown on her smooth, fleshy face, Sister Angelica had shown us how it was done. She'd given each of us a gentle pinch on the spot where the devout frown should be. We had practiced marching in the schoolyard. Sister Angelica had hummed in slow four-four time.

"Yadadeeda, dadadeeda. Yadadeeda, dadadeeda. Keep your place and close the gap. Keep your place and close the gap. Yadadeeda, dadadeeda!"

Saint Rosa's Day was overcast, and there was hardly any wind. A storm was brewing. The altar boys led the way, swinging their censers, which left a trail of small clouds of spicy, pungent holy smoke. Then came the Sisters, whose thin, high-pitched prayers alternated with the low voices of the parish priest and the Franciscan monks. The Bishop, under his canopy, which was carried by four acolytes, came next. We followed.

In Put Street, we walked over the colored-sand pictures of the Holy Virgin and Rosa of Lima.

"Yadadeeda, dadadeeda," Sister Angelica hummed softly, but she herself was rather out of step. Her pink face shone with excitement.

We passed the small house altars and the bishop blessed them one by one. We left the town through the Putse Gate. Step by step, we came closer to the Kollenberg hill, where the chapel of our homesick saint stood. High above us, the linden trees rustled. We went past the roadside Stations of the Cross, including the Garden of Gethsemane, all built of brick. Van Wessum's bricks.

"Yadadeeda, dadadeeda."

I noticed that Muulke had hiked up her dress because she was stepping on the hem. And I saw Jess looking radiant as she held her head up high and kept her back straight.

The button-chewer had wrought another miracle.

Two weeks after the Crocodile's stories had been blown all over Sjlammbams Sahara, Oompah Hatsi had disappeared. He wasn't in the cemetery, he wasn't hiding in the hedge, and no trace of him was to be found in the town, either. He seemed to have vanished into thin air.

Thirty good cigars had vanished from the workshop, too. But that wasn't all.

"I'll be!" Dad exclaimed.

Our brothers scratched their heads, perplexed.

In the workshop windows sat the fly screens. That is to say, the frames of the fly screens. The wire netting itself was gone.

"What on earth does he want with that?" Sjeer said.

And Piet suggested that crazies would always be crazies.

We couldn't make heads or tails of it, until we found the burlap sack on a chair in a corner of the living room. A sheet of paper was pinned to the sack with the inscription, in small, graceful letters: FOR JESS.

Dad was amazed. "Did you know he could write?"

When Jess carefully opened the sack and removed what hid inside, we all breathed in at the same time.

Oompah had removed the netting from the screens so he could stretch it over wire frames to make fealther-light, delicate wings. They were beautifully symmetrical and the netting itself had been delicately embroidered in mother-of-pearl, sky blue, and gold.

And so Jess got to be an angel after all.

The people watching the procession were rather baffled by the new Mary, who was stuck in a papier-mâché grotto that was far too small for her. On her head sat a coronet that didn't fit, and in her hands she carried a somewhat creased cardboard heart-of-love.

"There is no help for it," Mother Superior had said despairingly a week before. "I really can't let her go as an angel. She's practically bald on one side. We'll just have to let her be Mary. Then she can at least cover her head."

"Hail Mary, full of grace," we prayed. "Protect us against contagious diseases." And Muulke, who made sure she kept up with the Blessed Virgin Mary's float, muttered with a grin, "And against bald spots on our heads."

Fat Tonnie looked furious but couldn't do anything. She knew better.

The day after we had found Jess again, Oma Mei had filled her basket with leeks, potatoes, and cucumbers from the vegetable garden and had told me to come with her. We went to one of the worst, most foul-smelling slums in the town. The narrow streets were slippery with filth. I had to go and apologize to Tonnie.

"And while I think of it, Tonnie," our grandmother had said, her voice gentle as a spring breeze, after handing the basket of vegetables to Tonnie's mother, "if you ever lay a hand on my Jess again, I'll come and lay a hand on you. And I won't stop till you're as bald as a tadpole. Understood?"

Oma Mei didn't even come up to Fat Tonnie's shoulders, but her spinning swivel-eye and the seriousness of her words had obviously gotten through.

The procession was over. Muulke wrestled herself out of her wings before we even got to the bottom of the Kollenberg hill. Jess kept hers on until I could carefully undo them outside the church, where they would be kept for the following year. Dad helped me.

"Dad," I said softly.

"Yes, *leeveke*?"

"Have all the cigars been sold?"

"They sure have."

"So are we rich now?"

He grinned. "Don't you worry about that, *leeveke*. We're at least rich enough to keep the bank out of our hair for a while." And he winked.

It started to rain. Fat drops came down from the sky, and seconds later the thunderstorm broke.

We ran to the market square—Oma Mei, Dad, our brothers, Muulke, Jess, and I.

"If that isn't our new cigar king," shouted Nol.

He beckoned. We went to where the cigar kings and the cigar emperor were sheltering close together under the awning of the Café Lejeune.

The kings greeted dad. They offered him a cigar from their own boxes. When he flushed, because he didn't know which one to choose and who to snub, they grinned at each other and suddenly looked an awful lot like our brothers.

The cigar emperor said nothing, but he nodded when Dad greeted him. His felt hat was just as immaculate as it had been in winter.

Conversation got underway while the rain drummed on the awning.

Jess, Muulke, and I just stood there.

"Stand up straight," said Oma Mei.

The cigar emperor's wife was there, too. Her face was powdered and her eyebrows had been plucked into two thin lines, but close up she looked more normal than from a distance. She dabbed her face with her handkerchief, nodded to us, and winced at every thunderclap.

"It can't be easy for you," she said to Oma Mei. Her voice was soft and a little husky. "Three growing young ladies." Muulke burst out laughing.

"And don't forget the four gentlemen," said Oma Mei, after giving Muulke a withering look. "And one cigar king."

And then she said it. I don't know if she was aware of it herself, but I heard it, and so did Muulke and Jess.

"And all the while I'm already standing with one foot in my grave," she said.

For some calculations, we didn't need our brothers. Perhaps it was Dad standing among the cigar kings smiling from ear to ear, and for the first time looking as if he belonged somewhere. Or perhaps it was simply because someone had been willing to listen to her story.

At any rate, something had made Oma Mei take half a step back, and after the miraculous changing of useless cigars into good cigars, and the miracle of Jess becoming an angel after all, perhaps this was the greatest miracle of them all.

The Opposite of Worrying [3]

ON THE MONDAY OF the last week of our summer vacation, we rode the bus to Dad's town. We sat together on the seat at the back, watching the landscape glide by. It was a warm late-summer's day, and a breeze blew through the half-open windows. I could smell diesel, sweat, and Oma Mei's eau de cologne.

Our brothers were pointing out cars and scoring points off each other with facts and figures about diesel engines and tire pressures. Muulke and Jess squabbled about who would sit by the window on the way back.

The only silent ones were our father and grandmother, who sat on the seat in front of us. Oma Mei was sitting very straight in her Sunday best. She wore the hat with the rose. The felt flower trembled in the breeze. She looked straight ahead. I saw the small rake sticking out of her basket.

Dad was looking out of the window. He nodded at the road, the trees, the houses. Perhaps it was an effect of the bumpy road, or perhaps he was greeting the things he hadn't seen in such a long time. I couldn't be sure.

After half an hour, the bus stopped at the station. There were only a few people out in the streets. It was already hot and the shops weren't open yet.

We had to walk for another half hour. As we got closer, everybody grew quieter. I tried to work out how long it was since we had been here, but for some reason I couldn't get the dates straight in my head.

It was a small cemetery. There was no tall hedge to protect it, only a ridiculously low wall you could simply step over. But we went across to the small entry gate with its well-oiled hinges all the same.

Our mother's headstone was of unpolished stone, so it wasn't shiny, but her grave was beautifully maintained.

MARIA THEODORA ANTONIA SOFIA BOON-KLEIN

APRIL 17, 1903–OCTOBER 10, 1928

ANTONIUS HUBERTUS WILHELMINA MARGARETHA BOON

NOVEMBER 3, 1900–

I recognized Oma Mei's hand in the way the pebbles had been raked, and in the small rosebush growing alongside the low pergola that contained, but also protected it.

"I think you were going to prove that children are perfectly capable of behaving properly in a cemetery," Oma Mei said.

Muulke and I went to get water. Our brothers and Jess helped with the weeding.

Of course it was silly for nine of us to try to clean that simple grave all together. We were constantly in each other's way, but we were very careful not to complain, or giggle, or make stupid remarks. We were determined to prove that we were perfectly capable.

Dad did nothing, and even that looked as if it was hard for him. He stood on one leg, then shifted to the other. He chewed the inside of his cheek, laughed when he noticed I was looking at him, and finally walked off, his face crumpling.

I looked from Dad to my mother's grave, not knowing what to do.

"He'll come back," said Oma Mei, without looking up. "Just leave him be for a while."

Carefully, she snipped a couple of wilted blooms from the rose bush.

Perhaps the thought came to me because we were standing there in a cemetery.

"Oma?"

"Yes, *kendj*?"

"Where is Charley's grave?"

She stood up with a groan. "Charley's grave?"

"I know where Nienevee's grave is, but where is Charley's?"

"Nobody knows exactly."

"What do you mean?"

She handed me the shriveled roses. They crackled in my hands.

"Even graves aren't forever, *leeveke*. After Nienevee died, there was nobody to look after Charley's grave. Some years later, when money was due for his plot, there was no one to pay it. So the Council cleared the grave and deposited the bones in the ossuary."

I looked at my mother's grave and at her name and Dad's.

Suddenly, I no longer thought their names being next to each other was spooky. Not quite so spooky, anyway.

Oma Mei had been right. Dad did come back. His face was almost back to normal, and his voice hardly wavered.

"She rests in the loveliest spot in the world," he said.

Oma Mei dusted down her dress and inspected the grave, shielding her eyes from the sun with her hand.

"But it's a long way away," she said.

"But it's so lovely here," said Dad.

"But it's a long way away."

Their voices weren't angry. They spoke more as if they were travelers, each in a different spot in the world, each at a different place in time. And the only way to find each other was to listen to each other and to keep on listening, again and again.

"So," said Oma Mei, when the gravestone had been scrubbed, the letters of our mother's name had been cleaned, the rose bush pruned, the weeds pulled, and fresh flowers put in the vase.

She packed up her basket. In her hand, she held the rag she had used for cleaning. "A rag for her rag-doll heart," she said, carefully folding it into quarters and putting it away.

On the way back, I sat on the wide rear seat of the bus again, squashed between my brothers and sisters. And again, I smelled the scent of diesel, sweat, and eau de cologne, but this time I smelled something else, too. Something that wasn't anything in particular that gave off a scent: the scent of time to come.

The opposite of worrying had finally arrived.